The Cat's Pajamas

A Charming and Clever Compendium of Feline Trivia

By Leonore Fleischer

Designed by Gloria Adelson

HARPER & ROW, PUBLISHERS, New York

Cambridge, Philadelphia, San Francisco, London
Mexico City, São Paulo, Sydney

Typography by Gerard Associates Phototypesetting, Inc.

Special thanks to Mimi Vang Olsen for the use of the drawing on page 106 from her book *The Cat Lover's Book of Days* (Harper & Row, 1982).

Director of Research: David Frankel

FIRST EDITION

Design by Lulu Graphics

ISBN: 0-06-090974-9
Library of Congress Catalog Card Number: 82-47907

82 83 84 85 86 10 9 8 7 6 5 4 3 2 1

HUDSON

LULU

KITTY

OLIVER

HONEY

DANIEL

MITZI

SNEAKER

 **ACKNOWLEDGMENTS**

The idea for this book originated with Edward L. Burlingame, the publisher of the Harper & Row Trade Books Division. This suggestion seemed surprising coming from someone who had never professed an interest in cats, but when asked he replied: "I *love* cats. I even think we have one at home."

LARRY ASHMEAD

The author wishes to give special thanks to Barbara A. Bannon, Phyllis Levy and Laura Torbet for their contributions to this book. And, of course, to Larry Ashmead, a great editor, and to Mitzi and her pals for sitting on the galley pages while she was reading them.

LEONORE FLEISCHER

The designer of this book wishes to thank Amaretti, Barney, Bodoni, Blumchen, Charley, Cleo, Copy, Chulita, Daisy, Dusty, Foxy, George, Gudrun, Hudson, The Maiser, Pooh, Punky, Samantha 1 and Samatha 2, Spider, Sunshine, Toutou, Zazie; and honorary cats (i.e., dogs): Amy, Annie, Balthazar, Kumo, Lucy, Molly; and one bird: Tea Cake. Lulu with tired paws called out for turkey club and never forgot the Russian dressing.

GLORIA ADELSON

The Cat's Pyjamas: Something superlatively good; first rate; attractive. An American colloquialism in use by 1900 and current in England in the 1920s and 1930s.

> —*Brewer's Dictionary of*
> *Phrase and Fable*
> (Harper & Row, 1970)

It's a good poem,
It's the cat's pajamas.
> —*The Plastic Age, by Percy Marks*
> (Century, 1924)

The drawing above was designed by "Kat" Doty for The Cat's Pyjamas, 20 Church St., Montclair, N.J. 07042.

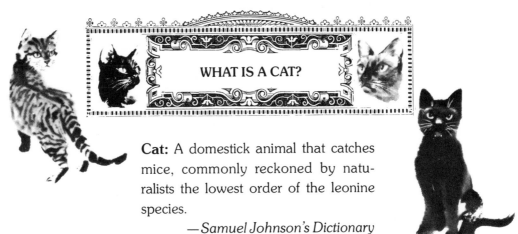

WHAT IS A CAT?

Cat: A domestick animal that catches mice, commonly reckoned by naturalists the lowest order of the leonine species.

—*Samuel Johnson's Dictionary*

The Oxford English Dictionary says that a cat is "a well-known carnivorous quadruped *(Felis domesticus)* which has long been domesticated, being kept to destroy mice, and as a house pet."

Webster's Third New International Dictionary defines the cat as "a long-domesticated carnivore mammal that is usually regarded as a distinct species *(Felis catus,* syn. *Felis domestica),* though probably ultimately derived by selection from among the hybrid progeny of several small Old World wildcats (as the Kaffir cat and the European wild cat), that occurs in several varieties distinguished chiefly by length of coat, body form, and presence or absence of tail, and that makes a pet valuable in controlling rodents and other small vermin but tends to revert to a feral state if not housed and cared for." All very well, even if the British think of the cat in the Latin masculine *(domesticus)* and the Americans in the feminine *(domestica).* If you are to believe the dictionaries, a cat is little more than a fur-bearing exterminator, a Mouse-No-More, or a Rat-Away. But in fact no dictionary touches on the essential nature of the cat.

What is a cat? A cat is a purring parcel of paradox, a cunning collection of contradictions. A cat is lazy and busy, dainty and savage, affectionate and aloof, greedy and finicky, sound asleep in one instant, and awake and stalking in the next. A cat is a limp puddle of softness, surrounding a steel-hard and ever-alert set of muscles. A cat is a priceless piece of porcelain, and a rag doll sprawling on its back, begging for a tummy scratch, paws asprawl. A cat is better than you are, more honest, more graceful, smarter for her size, better coordinated and infinitely more beautiful. A cat has the face of a pansy flower, and is just as velvety. A cat holds infinity in her eyes, and your heart in her front paws. The paws themselves are yet another feline paradox—the softest velvet sheathing the sharpest daggers.

A cat is complex, with complex emotions and characteristics. One is obstinacy. If you are evil enough to ruffle the fur of your freshly washed cat, you'll see her start again, the whole elaborate, laborious ritual, back to Hair One. If you are reading a large newspaper, all spread out on the table, your cat will come and sit on the very paragraph you are reading, the talented cat draping her tail with miraculous precision over the very *line* you're not finished with. Catch a dog in your favorite chair, and he slinks away abashed. The cat will pretend incomprehension; surely you must know it's *her* chair? *No* means everything to a dog, nothing to a cat.

A cat is restfulness; it's impossible not to relax in the presence of a dozing cat. When you watch a cat licking herself clean, time stands still. The best tranquilizer in the world is the soft monotony of the purr, and a cat purring on your lap is a somnolent invitation to Dreamland.

Above all, a cat is love. A cat brings you gifts: half a lizard, an eviscerated squirrel, but she means well. She brings you also the gift of herself, the gift of her preference for you, the sight of you, your scent, the sound of your voice, the touch of your hand. When you're special to a cat, you're special indeed. Of course, she rarely comes right out and says so. She just *happens* to stroll casually into a room when you're in it; she just *happens* to wander out again when you leave; choice or preference have nothing to do with it. Oh, is that *your* hand I'm licking? Sorry, thought it was my own paw.

The kinked tail is not exclusive to the Siamese cat, but occurs in other Eastern breeds, notably those of Burma and Malaya.

The Manx is not the only tailless cat; they exist in Japan and in the Crimea, and in many other parts of the Far East.

Cats are designed very efficiently to be hunting animals. Digitigrade, they walk on their toes, and silently, because their claws are retractile; they can be drawn up into the sheath or extended as the cat needs them. This makes cats very light of foot and noiseless in their approach to their prey.

The raspiness of a cat's tongue is caused by the *papillae* on its surface, which enable the cat to clean its fur thoroughly so that it emits no odor to scare off prey. The papillae are also used in licking flesh from bones when the cat has made a kill.

The facial whiskers, or *vibrissae,* are sensitive, because they are connected to nerve endings and grow from a special type of follicle. Even the whiskers on a cat's front legs, the carpal hairs, are highly sensitive to touch. Cats evidently use their facial whiskers for perception, particularly of close objects, narrow gaps, and in dim light.

The wild cat *(Felis silvestris)* is now extinct in most parts of Europe, although it is still found in Scotland. Although it appears larger than the domestic cat, the skeletons are the same size; it's the long hair and bushy tail of the wild cat that give it more bulk. The lower jaw of the wild cat has a shorter gap between the canine teeth and the premolars than the domesticated cat has. The teeth of the domesticated cat are smaller, too.

Mammals, including humans, can distinguish among four tastes only: sweet, salt, bitter, and acid. Cats are unique in that they apparently do not react to sweet at all, but instead are extremely sensitive to the taste of water. Since the nasal passages of a cat open directly into its mouth, the senses of smell and taste are linked closely together. Cats also have a third sense, missing in man, which is centered in the roof of the mouth in an organ called the Jacobson's organ after its discoverer. When the Jacobson's organ is stimulated by something as powerful as sex musk or catnip, the cat will press its tongue against the roof of its mouth, in a facial gesture called the flehmen reaction.

A six-pound cat has a normal heartbeat of 240 beats per minute. Compare this with a 145-pound human, whose heart beats at the rate of 75 beats per minute, and a bird like the blue titmouse, weighing only a couple of ounces, whose heartbeat is an alarming 960 to the minute.

He loves me!
He loves me not!
He loves me!

Sex and the single cat: The word "cat" has long been synonymous with randiness and sexual potency (as in "tomcatting around" or "like a cat in heat"), deservedly so, as anybody who owns an unspayed female or a philandering male can tell you. The tomcat is particularly aggressive in mating season, and the female in her cycle meows piteously and caterwauls for a mate. Yet the mating of cats leaves much to be desired from the human point of view, because it's brief (although frequent, when the female is in estrus) and evidently somewhat painful. Not only does the male grab the female's neck harshly in his jaws when he mounts her from behind, but there is a set of backward-pointing stiff barbs on his penis that hurt her when he withdraws, which is almost immediately. Anyway, the female lets out a shriek as soon as the act is over, but that may be as much due to frustration as to pain. Cats don't cuddle before, during, or after sex; the act is all business and little pleasure. Nor have they been known to light up cigarettes.

HISSING AND SPITTING DEPARTMENT

In medieval France, in Aix-en-Provence, a horrible ritual was followed on Corpus Christi day. A male cat was wrapped in swaddling clothes and shown to the people for their veneration, as a stand-in for the infant Jesus. Then, at noon, the miserable cat was burned alive in a ceremonial sacrifice.

From *The Devil's Dictionary,* by Ambrose Bierce: "**Cat,** n.: A soft, indestructible automaton provided by nature to be kicked when things go wrong in the domestic circle."

In pre-Elizabethan England, a cat was sometimes enclosed in a bag, or firkin, or leather bottle, and hung up in a tree so that archers could use it as a target. Shakespeare mentions this "sport" in *Much Ado About Nothing:* "Hang me in a bottle like a cat."

In the 1930s, when the New York Aquarium was at the Battery, cats were used to keep the rat population in check. The rats used to perch on top of the fish tanks and fish for fish. But the cats also fished for fish, so Dr. Christopher Coates, then aquarist, trained the cats to dislike fish by giving them little shocks with the electric eel. When an aquarium cat pounced on the eel, it would get ten volts or so, which soon cured the cat of going fishing.

Three harmful myths have cost the cat dear—first, that it has contributed to Sudden Infant Death Syndrome (SIDS) or "crib death," by suffocating the infant in its crib. The latest research points to a hormonal imbalance in the infant dating to pregnancy. Second, that cats suck your breath from your body when you are sleeping. Cats do love to sleep with humans, because we are warm and cuddly. I sleep with my cat, nose to nose, but it is more likely I suck her breath than she mine. Third, it is thought that cats cause human leukemia. Although they can transmit feline leukemia to one another, it is not human leukemia, and no shred of evidence says it is.

In 1950, M. Pierre Pflimlin, French Minister of Agriculture, issued a decree whereby any cat wandering more than two hundred meters from home was to be regarded as a "wild cat" and treated accordingly—in other words, shot. A French animal protection society, immediately up in arms, called upon the Council of State to revoke the decree and to prosecute Pflimlin for passing an illegal ordinance; the society claimed the minister had violated articles 454 and 483 of the penal code, making him liable to a 12,000-franc fine, and eight days in jail. Ten days after the decree was issued, Pflimlin was forced to resign, officially over an issue involving the price of sugar beets; unofficially, purrs of approval were heard all over France.

In the sixteenth century a nameless inventor proposed to use cats in the then current version of chemical warfare. What this dastard intended was to attach "small cannon charged with pestilential odors" to the backs of cats and send them among the enemy, but only provided the enemy was not Christian. There is no record that this plan was ever put into effect.

The United States Army in 1959 was in the process of developing a gas that appeared to reduce "the will to fight." The army showed a film of a cat who, having inhaled the gas, was running from a mouse.

In a letter to *The New York Times,* January 22, 1975, Edward Lindemann, a science editor, suggested that in our debate and concern over diminishing food sources we have omitted an important edible animal, the stray cat. He also suggested that we consider as food sources the dog, the horse, and the termite (evidently the termite is 45 percent protein).

CAT SUPERSTITIONS AROUND THE WORLD

Another old Chinese belief: A cat washing its face means a stranger is coming.

The Chinese say that the end of a cat's nose is always cold, but for one day during summer (the summer solstice, June 21, the longest day of the year) the cat's nose becomes warm. That is why the cat dreads cold but loves heat.

One old Russian superstition says that if you want to be happy in your new home, a cat must move in with you. Another states that when you bring a new cat or kitten into your home, you must throw her immediately on to the bed. If she begins to wash herself and settles on the bed, she will stay with you. Another Eastern European custom is to butter a new cat's paws. The idea is that a cat will stay with you if she washes herself, and the butter is to induce her to lick her paws.

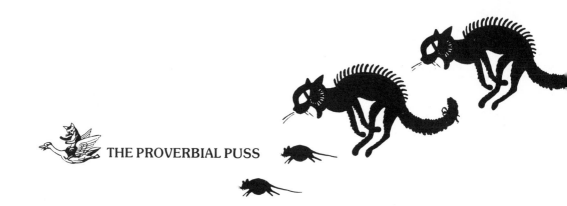

THE PROVERBIAL PUSS

The cat has entered human language in a multitude of proverbs, expressions, adages, epigrams, phrases, maxims, metaphors, and similes. We say, "like a cat on a hot tin roof," when we mean someone is nervous; we say, "no room even to swing a cat," when we mean tight quarters (Smollett used the phrase back in 1771); we say "to let the cat out of the bag" when we tell secrets; we say "raining cats and dogs," "when the cat's away, the mice will play," "to set the cat among the pigeons," and so on, and everybody knows what we mean. The French say, *"appeler un chat un chat,"* or "call a cat a cat," as we say about a spade. We say, "let sleeping dogs lie," but the French say *"N'eveillez pas le chat qui dort,"* or "don't wake a sleeping cat." The Italians say, *"Non fu mai cacciator gatto che miagola,"* or "A cat who mews is not a good hunter." My grandmother used to say sarcastically in Yiddish, *"M'schict der katz noch pitter,"* or "one sends the cat out to buy butter," which is the equivalent of leaving the fat kid in charge of the candy store. In other parts of the world, the expression is, "don't send the cat out to get lard," but since lard is pig fat, my grandmother would turn in her grave if she heard that.

And we say, when something is absolutely top-notch, that it's the cat's meow, or the cat's whiskers or, you betcha, the cat's pajamas.

Herewith the proverbial puss:

"Touch not the cat but with a glove" is the motto of the Mackintosh clan of Scotland, and on the subject of gloves, "A gloved cat catches no mice" is a very old adage turning up in many languages, as is "as clumsy as a cat in mittens."

"The cat is hungry when a crust contents her."

"If you leave the kitchen door open, don't blame the cat for stealing meat." Also its corollary, "Every cat is honest when the meat's put away in the larder."

"An old cat eats as much as a young one."

"To fight like Kilkenny cats" means to fight until the bitter end for both sides. There's a particularly gruesome anecdote connected with this: some Hessian mercenaries, garrisoned in Kilkenny during the Irish Rebellion of 1798, tied a couple of cats together by their tails and set them to fighting. When they were ordered to stop, one man cut the tails off with a stroke of his sword. The cats ran off, leaving the tails behind, and the soldiers claimed that the cats had destroyed each other, right down to their tails.

"It's enough to make the cat speak" usually means that the booze is prime stuff, and will set your tongue to wagging.

A Scottish proverb: "It's easy to teach the cat the way to the churn" (where cream is turned into butter).

A Spanish proverb: *"Los amores del gato riñendo entran."* The cat's amatory adventures start off with the showing of teeth.

"To live under the cat's foot," as a mouse does under the tyranny of the cat's paw.

"When all the candles are out, the cat is grey."
(John Heywood, *Proverbs*, 1546).

Curiosity may have killed the cat, but satisfaction brought it back.

Cat and the Fiddle: Not only is the phrase in the popular nursery rhyme, but it's also a common inn sign in England, where a large number of pubs and inns are called "The Cat and Fiddle." Possibly it derives from the French *"le chat infidel,"* or "the unfaithful cat." At any rate, "Cat and Kittens" on an inn sign usually means that large and small pewter measures of beer are (or were) served there.

"A cat may look at a king" means: "I may be below you on the social or economic ladder, but I'm as good as you are." In 1652, a political pamphlet with this title was published in England.

Here's a gem from upstate New York: "The cat's fur makes the kitten's britches. Ever seen 'em on a hen?" Translation: "Don't ask me silly questions, and I won't give you silly answers."

A Dutch proverb: "Those who don't like cats won't get handsome mates."

Old adage, quoted by Lady Macbeth: "All cats love fish but fear to wet their feet." The meaning is clear—those who want something badly enough should be willing to take some risk to obtain it.

To switch sides, or to cleverly reverse the order of things so as to make the worse argument appear the better, is called "turning the cat in the pan."

A German proverb: "The cat who frightens the mice away is as good as the cat who eats them."

Another Scottish proverb: "A timid cat makes a bold mouse."

"Before the cat can lick its ear" means, of course, never.

A Japanese proverb: "The borrowed cat catches no mice."

A French proverb: "A man who loves cats will marry an immoral woman."

A French proverb: *"C'est mal acheter de chat en sac,"* or "It's a bad thing to buy a cat in a bag," the old pig-in-a-poke metaphor.

From the Latin, eleventh century: *"Ad cuius veniat scit catus lingere barbam."* The cat knows whose beard she licks.

More about the phrase "the cat's pajamas"—it dates from a time when pajamas, like wristwatches, were still considered daring and unconventional masculine attire (the nightshirt and the pocket watch having ruled supreme for generations) and is also one of the several popular 1920s catchphrases involving animals — *the bee's knees,* for example, or *the gnu's shoes,* or *the clam's garters.* (The clam's garters?)

From England: "Singing cats and whistling girls will come to a bad end."

From Japan: "When the cat mourns the mouse, you need not take her seriously."

An Arab proverb: "A cat that is always crying catches no mice."

Although it was long believed, and written many times, that a cheetah's claws, unlike those of every other member of the cat family, were not retractable, in fact, they are. But they lack the sheath that every other kind of cat possesses, and so it seems at first glance that they don't retract.

An old belief had it that a cat or dog would not drown as long as it could see the shore.

As for the old adage of using a cat's paw to pull your chestnuts out of the fire, it is possible that it arose through a misunderstanding. The Latin word *catellus* actually means "puppy," and in the earlier forms of the saying, a dog was the owner of the paw, not the cat.

The fable of the mice belling the cat was mentioned as far back as William Langland's *Piers Plowman* in the fourteenth century.

In Old Saxony, Henry the Fowler dictated that a fine of sixty bushels of corn be paid by anybody killing a cat which could still catch mice.

In certain heart diseases, the thrill felt over the region of the heart is known as the cat's purr.

A cat—black or not—crossing one's path was considered bad luck even as far back as classical Greece, and was mentioned by Aristophanes and Theophrastus.

THE CAT CALENDAR:
GREAT MOMENTS IN FELINE HISTORY

A.D. 936 — The Welsh pass laws for the safekeeping of cats, since cats protected food from rodents.

A.D. 999 — The first litter of kittens born in Japan is born in the Imperial palace at Kyoto.

A.D. 1602 — A law is passed in Japan ordering cats to be released from their leashes so that they can attack the rodents who were damaging the silk industry. Until then, cats were kept on leashes in Japan, as they were in China.

1604: King Henry IV of France issues a royal decree forbidding the barbarous living sacrifice of innocent cats by fire in "celebration" of St. John's Day. Before then, thousands of cats perished miserably all over France every year.

A.D. 1750 — Cats are officially imported into the American Colonies in order to control rodents.

1871: The first major cat show in Great Britain is held at the Crystal Palace, beginning a Golden Age of Cats.

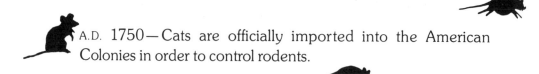

1871: A Siamese cat, "Mrs. Poodles," is exhibited at an English cat show for the first time. It received a lot of interest, but no great reviews. One journalist called it "a nightmare." In those days Siamese were rounder and heavier; breeders have turned them into the streamlined Deco numbers we know and love today. Not much later than that, the first Siamese cat was introduced into the United States by Mrs. Rutherford B. Hayes, wife of the President.

1895 — The first separate cat show in America was organized by an Englishman named Hyde, and proved an immediate success, creating much interest in cats in this country.

1899 — The first American cat club was founded, the Beresford Cat Club of Chicago, named for Lady Marcus Beresford of England, a great cat fancier who did much to improve American breeds.

1901: The first Manx Club was formed in Great Britain.

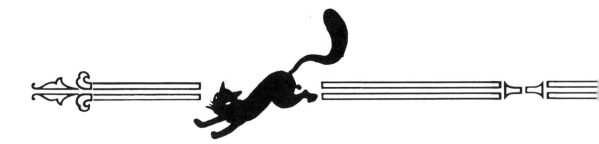

1942: Captain Midnight, a black cat owned by an American family, was transported to wartime England from Pennsylvania, where it was transferred to a bomber. The red-white-and-blue label on the cat carrier described Captain Midnight as a "special envoy." His mission: to be flown over Germany until he had crossed the path of Adolf Hitler and brought him bad luck, a sort of paws-across-the-seas patriotic gesture with a palpable air of propawganda about it.

1948: Food supplies being scarce in war-torn Europe, the United States held a Cats for Europe campaign, rounding up American alley cats by the thousands and shipping them to France to protect food shipments from mice and rats. Afterward, these cats could not be kept down on the farm, for they'd seen Paree.

September, 1971: D. E. Gordon Oltman is elected to the Student Senate of Southern Illinois University. Oltman, a cat, ran on a platform of expanded rat control and the solving of the dogs-on-campus problem. Diane E. Oltman, Gordon's owner, put her pet's name on the ballot to prove that students paid no attention at all to the candidates they voted for in student elections.

1971: The first Scottish Fold kitten, a mutation, was born to a farm cat, Susie, in Scotland. With its round face, round eyes, and floppy, folded-over ears, the Fold is the latest breed to catch the fancy of the fancy.

1973: Governor Ronald Reagan of California signs a bill into state law that can send a person to prison for kicking and injuring another person's cat.

1977: The Voice for Animals Society gives Amy Carter's Siamese cat Misty the title of First Feline. Her puppy Grits is dubbed First Canine and Vice-President Walter Mondale's collie Bonnie is named Vice-Canine.

December 7, 1981: *Time* magazine devotes its cover story to the cat and its influence in the American home, an acknowledgment that cats are where it's at for millions of us.

In China, cats were used to keep away the rats that ate the silkworms, hence cats were considered the guardians of the precious worms, and even the picture of a cat, placed on the wall of the room where silkworms were kept, was considered a powerful enough charm to keep the worms safe.

At the turn of the century, the Quincy House in Boston had a large yellow cat named Jack, whose portrait hung in the office. Jack in the flesh would enter the dining room at mealtime and take his place at an empty table. A waiter would move Jack's chair up to the table and bring in a dish of sliced meat, and Jack would place his paws on the table and eat his dinner with perfect manners, before making a dignified departure.

The office of the famous New York *Sun* (a great newspaper, now defunct) always had a complement of working cats, and Charles Henry Dana, the paper's gifted publisher, described the publishing pussy thus: "*Sun* office cat *(Felis Domestica; var. Journalistica)*. The habitat of the species is in Newspaper Row; its lair is in the *Sun* building, its habits are nocturnal, and it feeds on discarded copy and anything else of a pseudo-literary nature upon which it can pounce. A single member of this family has been known to devour three and a half columns of presidential possibilities, seven columns of general politics, pretty much all but the head of a railroad accident, and a full page of miscellaneous news. The progenitrix of the family arrived in the *Sun* office many years ago, and within a few short months had noticeably raised the literary tone of the paper, as well as a large and vociferous family of kittens. Just before her death — immediately before, in fact — the mother cat developed a literary taste of her own and drank the contents of an ink bottle. She was buried with literary honors, and one of her progeny was advanced to the duties and honors of office cat." Of the then incumbent, Dana wrote, "Grown to cat-hood, he is a creditable specimen of his family, with beryl eyes, beautiful striped fur, showing fine mottlings of mucilage and ink, a graceful and aspiring tail, an appetite for copy unsurpassed in the annals of his race. . . ."

CATS AND CELEBRITIES

King Edward VII of England had several pet cats. His mother, Queen Victoria, owned two Blue Persian cats whom she cherished. After her death, her precious White Heather remained in the Royal Family with Edward VII.

Winston Churchill's ginger cat used to sit in on wartime cabinet meetings. Churchill was passionately fond of cats, and the Savoy Hotel in London boasts a large statue of a black cat, in memory of the great Prime Minister and beloved statesman. In the Pinafore Room, of which Sir Winston used to be an habitué, if a party of thirteen wishes to be seated, the statue is seated in the fourteenth chair, to avoid the bad luck that comes with thirteen at table. The cat itself is thought to be lucky, as well.

When the piano virtuoso Ignace Paderewski gave his first London performance at the St. James Theatre in 1890, he saw the theater cat sitting on stage in full view of the audience as he walked on. "Wish me luck," he whispered to him, whereupon the cat jumped into his lap and purred "in concert pitch" until the end of the first selection. The concert was a resounding success. Afterward, in the green room, Paderewski played to invited guests Scarlatti's *Cat Fugue,* a piece inspired by Scarlatti's cat walking on the keys of his piano.

SHORT TAKES

In Rome at the turn of the century cat owners were able to subscribe to a cat-meat service. Butchers' men would drive through the city daily in carts stacked with cat meat, calling a distinctive cry to summon subscribers' cats, who were then fed. What prevented the common run of nonsubscribing cats from running up when the cart came round and claiming their share, we are not told. But we can't quite picture the street cat, tough and smart, letting the privileged cats get away with all the livers and lights.

35

When Sir Henry Wyat was imprisoned in the Tower of London by Richard III for his Lancastrian sympathies during the Wars of the Roses, he was being systematically starved, and existed on the barest minimum of food until a cat began bringing him pigeons down the chimney. Although the gaoler was forbidden to give Wyat food, he wasn't forbidden to cook for him, and so he prepared the cat's pigeons, thus saving Wyat's life. Wyat was later released. A very similar story is told about the third earl of Southampton, Henry Wriothesley, and his imprisonment. All of which leads us to believe that the poor cats in the legends were in fact bringing their own dinners down the chimney when they were intercepted and deprived of their pigeons.

During the siege of Leningrad, a cat named Mourka (many Russian cats are named Mourka; the name is derived from the Russian word for purring) made her way nightly across the Nazi gun emplacements outside the city. She was, in fact, carrying messages from the besieged city to a house outside the lines. There, at least, she was given a good dinner.

Faith, the stray who became the resident cat of St. Paul's Church in Watling Street, London, for twelve years, died in 1948, and a plaque to her memory was dedicated in St. Augustine and St. Faith's Chapel, beneath the church. Faith has been called "the bravest cat in the world," because, during the Blitz in 1940, Faith remained in a burning building, refusing to leave her kitten. The plaque was donated by the People's Dispensary for Sick Animals of the Poor, in honor of Faith's "steadfast courage in the Battle of Britain." Her funeral service, held at Holy Trinity Church, included an open invitation for the local children to bring their pets. The service was attended by dozens of cats, kittens, ducks, chickens, guinea pigs, a lamb, a white mouse, twenty horses, a Pekingese, a bull mastiff, and a minnow in a jar.

A tomcat named Fat Albert was the official blood donor cat of the Marlton Animal Hospital in Marlton, New Jersey, in the early 1970s. Fat Albert, who arrived at the hospital as a beatup stray and was taken in by the hospital staff, gives blood to cats in need of a transfusion. He is the first member of the Pet Food Institute's Hall of Fame for Cats. Possibly he is the only member, since the P.F.I. offices in Chicago and Washington appear never to have heard of their Hall of Fame, and could not tell us what other cats were enshrined there. But Fat Albert, who died early in 1982, had the plaque to prove it. He is sorely missed.

THE CAT IN ANCIENT EGYPT

Sacred or sacrificed? Ever since Herodotus wrote of the mummified cats of ancient Egypt decked out in necklaces and earrings of gold and lapis lazuli, we have supposed that these cats were reverently buried after dying of natural causes. At the close of the nineteenth century, archaeological excavations in Egypt uncovered vast numbers of cat mummies, and at the turn of the century fifty-three such mummies were presented to the University of Pennsylvania Museum. Radioactive carbon dating showed that one of them dated to 380 B.C. and another to about 170 B.C. or pretty late in the Egyptian calendar. A close examination of the mummified remains revealed that only nine of the fifty-three cats were more than one year old at the time of their death, and that twenty-two were four months old or less. Seven of the cats, according to x-rays, had died of broken necks. The explanation, according to a report in the museum's journal, is that cats were raised specifically for the purpose of being killed and mummified as votive offerings, and sold to the public to be left at temples.

Cats are pictured in the tomb paintings of ancient Egypt, and by New Kingdom times (sixteenth century B.C. and later), the cat was not only domesticated but venerated, both as itself and in its godly manifestations:

Cats were embalmed, mummified, placed in cat-sized and cat-shaped sarcophagi, and either sent to Bubastis to be buried, or buried in other sacred cat cemeteries laid out along the banks of the Nile. In the tombs with them were often buried offerings, such as cat statuettes carved of gold and precious or semiprecious stones. Hundreds of thousands of Egyptians would make a pilgrimage to Bubastis in the spring, when the cycle of life begins anew. The rites of Bubastis were described by the Greek historian Herodotus (450 B.C.), who told how boats of women sailed along the Nile, playing music for the people to come out and dance in worship.

 When a cat died, the family it lived with went into mourning, shaving their eyebrows. When a house burned, it was more important to save the household cat than the household goods.

The Egyptian cat-goddess Pasht (also Bast or Bastet), was depicted with the head of a cat. Bast was the daughter of Isis, goddess of the earth and the moon, and Osiris, god of the sun and Isis' brother. The earliest image we have of her dates back to around 3,000 B.C. Her temple at her sacred city Bubastis housed sacred cats, but all cats, not only the sacred temple cats, were revered and protected. The killing of a cat was punishable by death.

The image of the cat was used to decorate jewelry, art, and other objects. Cats themselves were depicted wearing earrings and necklaces of gold and precious stones.

 On one occasion, when an Egyptian town was besieged by Persians, the Persian commander ordered live cats to be thrown over the city walls, knowing that the defenders would rather surrender their city than risk injury to the cats.

The cat, who sleeps curled up in a circle, was associated with the eternal circle of life. Also, the cat was identified with the sun god Ra; Egyptians believed that the cat's eyes caught the fire of the sun during the day and reflected it back at night, signifying that the sun would return the next morning. If a cat was killed, the solar and lunar gods would be angry, and the end of the world and eternal darkness became a distinct possibility. Bast is also the goddess of fire, and the cat was associated with fire through her because a cat's fur, when dry, gives off the sparks of static electricity.

Egyptians believed that the size of a cat's eyes waxed and waned with the moon and the tides. Bast was the goddess of the new moon.

In order to ensure the sunrise, the sun god Ra, in the form of a cat, fought the serpent of darkness, Apep, every night and killed him, although Apep always came back to life so that the battle could continue nightly. Eclipses of the sun were seen as great battles between Ra and Apep, the cat and the serpent, during which the Egyptians would run out into the street, shaking their sistrums to urge the cat on to kill the serpent.

The sistrum was a half-rattle, half-musical instrument, sacred to Isis and also to the cat, since the cat is a good mother, like the mother goddess Isis. The shape of the sistrum is the union of male and female, and presided over by the cat.

Because she killed the serpent Apep, the cat was believed to have the power to cure snakebite.

Cat mummies were so abundant in Egypt that in recent times an enterprising merchant from Manchester brought over a shipload of them to England, intending to sell them as fertilizer. Although the scheme did not bear fruit, many of the mummies found their way into museums in England and Europe.

CATS AND THE WEATHER

Sailors have many weather superstitions that are connected with cats. One old belief is that cats could raise storms with their tails, and a cat without a tail meant fair sailing weather. Hence, a Manx cat was considered the luckiest of all cats aboard ship. Other common beliefs held that one could forecast the weather by watching Puss's behavior. If she licked her fur the wrong way, hail was coming. A sneeze meant rain (this dates back to an old folktale about how the cat was called into being by the lion aboard Noah's Ark, who sneezed two cats out to combat the mice, who were ravaging the grain). The rain will come from the direction the cat's nose was pointing when it sneezed. A cat frisking on deck meant that a gale was due.

In Scotland there is a belief that when a cat scratches a table leg he raises a gale or the wind.

Japanese sailors believed that the tortoiseshell cat was the luckiest, and that one of them on board would give them warning of storms and keep away ghosts.

Some American beliefs about cats predicting the weather are: in eastern Kansas, a cat washing its face before breakfast forecasts rain. In New England, if a cat washes its face in the parlor, a shower; in Maine, if a cat scratches a fence, rain is due; in eastern Massachusetts, the face of a cat washing itself points in the direction from which the wind will come; in New York and Pennsylvania, a cat washing its face means clear weather (which is not only inconsistent but downright silly, because a healthy cat washes its face several times a day every day).

In Java, cats are bathed in pools to produce rain, and there are similar rituals in Sumatra.

Wives of English sailors would keep cats well-fed and happy so that they wouldn't wave their tails and thus raise gales at sea. On the Yorkshire coast, black cats became so expensive that sailors couldn't afford them.

Old English folk rhyme: "If the cat washes her face o'er the ear/'Tis a sign that the weather will be fine and clear."

Cat's-paws is the name for those little flutterings of water that indicate puffs of wind. These were thought by sailors to be the ghosts of ships' cats dancing before the wind.

An ancient belief is that if a cat, washing itself, puts her leg above her head, it's a sure sign that rain is on the way.

A CAT IN COURT

The British equivalent of Morris the Cat was a white cat named Arthur, who ate his cat food by scooping it out of the can with his paw and licking it off the paw, thus making him a natural star of TV commercials for cat food. In 1968, Arthur was signed by an outfit called Spillers Ltd. to be spokescat for its product, Kattemeat. And that's where the trouble began. Although Spillers claimed it bought Arthur outright from actor Tony Manning for $1,680, Manning protested that Arthur was only rented. The court ruled in favor of Spillers, but Manning refused to hand Arthur over, and was sent to jail for contempt of court. Before the iron gates closed on him, Manning stated that Arthur was safely out of the country, in the care of a friend, but Arthur was found later the same day at the home of TV talent agent Terence Gray, who says he discovered Arthur in a cardboard box on his doorstep. The case continued. Manning, still claiming to be the rightful owner, demanded $360,000 in damages from Spillers; he charged that Spillers Ltd. had caused some of Arthur's teeth to be extracted in order to encourage him to lick Kattemeat from his paw. Judge Nigel Bridge, presiding, examined Arthur's four remaining teeth as Arthur strolled along the judge's bench, tickled the cat under the chin, and, pronouncing Manning "the most brazen and unscrupulous liar I have ever heard testify from any witness box," awarded Arthur to Kattemeat.

✳ ✳ ✳ ✳ CATS AND CELEBRITIES ✳ ✳ ✳ ✳

The late Ethel Barrymore made a point of never going to see her own films. But she broke that rule when she went to see *Night Song* in 1948. Her role called for the use of a cat, and she employed her own silver tabby shorthair. Presumably, she wanted to watch Puss's performance.

Winston Churchill loved cats. On his eighty-eighth birthday, Churchill was presented with a cat by his friend Sir John "Jock" Colville, and he named it Jock. Jock lived at Chartwell, Churchill's famous home, and was most popular with visitors after the house was opened to the public. When Jock passed away in January of 1975, the curators of Chartwell had to replace him quickly with another cat named Jock, to keep the public happy. As a matter of fact, the new "Jock" was provided for in Churchill's will, which stipulated that a marmalade cat should be in comfortable residence at Chartwell forever and ever, and which left a sum of money to cover the cat's keep.

U.S. President Calvin Coolidge owned a canary named Caruso. Caruso developed a great fondness for a cat named Timmie, who belonged to a newspaper reporter named Bascom Timmins. Coolidge eventually had to make a present of Caruso to Timmons, or, rather, to Timmie. The bird would walk up and down the cat's back, and sit between his front paws. Caruso died one day while it was singing to the cat.

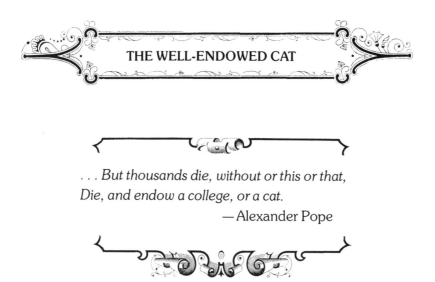

THE WELL-ENDOWED CAT

. . . But thousands die, without or this or that,
Die, and endow a college, or a cat.
—Alexander Pope

A famous harpist of seventeenth century France, Mme. Dupuis, inserted this clause in her will: "Item: I desire my sister, Marie Bluteau, and my niece, Madame Calonge, to look to my cats. If both cats should survive me, thirty *sous* a week must be laid out upon them, in order that they may live well. They are to be served daily, in a clean and proper manner, with two meals of meat soup, the same as we eat ourselves, but it is to be given them separately in two soup plates. The bread is not to be cut up into the soup, but must be broken into squares about the size of a nut, otherwise they will refuse to eat it. A ration of meat, finely minced, is to be added to it; the whole is then to be mildly seasoned, put into a clean pan, covered close, and carefully simmered before it is dished up. If only one cat should survive, half the sum mentioned will suffice."

Our John Paul Getty Award for Big Bucks goes to a pair of fifteen-year-old San Diego, California, cats named Hellcat and Brownie, whose owner died in 1963, leaving them both his estate of $415,000. There is no record of what the cats did with the inheritance. Did they invest it wisely or blow it on cream, caviar, and catnip? Or did the cats and their friends go to the Catskills?

Dr. William W. Grier, who died in June 1963, left $415,000 to his two cats for their lifetime, with the stipulation that George Washington University in the state of Washington receive the money after the death of the cats. Since neither of them survived their beloved master for long (one died in May, the other in July of 1965), the university did not have to wait long for the inheritance.

A Boston attorney, Woodbury Rand, bequeathed $40,000 to his pet cat Buster, cutting his relatives off without a penny because of "their cruelty to my cat." Buster died in 1945, intestate.

Mrs. Nettie Johnstown Huey died in 1955, leaving a fortune of $75,000 for her cat to be cared for in her home. On the pet's death in 1958, the money passed to Cornell University.

El-Daher-Beybars, the Sultan of Egypt and Syria, in A.D. 1280 bequeathed a garden in his will to be a haven for homeless cats called Ghet-el-Qoath ("the cats' orchard"). Other legacies left money for meat for the cats.

The richest cat in Chicago was Flat Nose, the last of the five cats owned by Mrs. Margaret Montgomery, who died in 1959, and who willed her entire estate of $24,000 to the cats for their lifetime. The will stipulated that Mrs. Montgomery's employee, William Fields, was to care for the cats with the income from the estate, and that their diet should include such delicacies as pot roast. Flat Nose, the longest-lived survivor, died in December of 1968, age 20, so he must have been getting his pot roast regularly.

An unnamed man left his property to endow a cat hospital in which an accordion "was to be played in the auditorium by one of the regular nurses, to be selected for that purpose exclusively, the playing to be kept up for ever and ever, without cessation day and night, in order that the cats may have the privilege of always hearing and enjoying that instrument which is the nearest approach to the human voice."

The French Cardinal Richelieu, who died in 1642, was passionately fond of cats. When he died, he left fourteen pet cats behind, and bequeathed an inheritance for their care, designating that the two servants who had fed and ministered to them during his lifetime should continue to do so. But the cats never lived to collect their inheritance; they were butchered by Swiss mercenaries and cooked into a stew.

The Manx cat was believed by sailors to be the luckiest of all cats aboard a ship, although the tortoiseshell puss ran her a close second.

How did the Manx cat lose its tail? One story goes that Irish invaders of the Isle of Man, where the cat originated, stole kittens' tails to wear in their helmets as plumes, yet other stories tell us that mother cats bit off their kittens' tails so that the Irish soldiers wouldn't get them.

How did the Manx cat lose its tail? It was the last animal to board the Ark, partly because it was out hunting mice and partly because a cat never comes when it's called. When the last animals had boarded two by two, the Manx turned up just as Noah was closing the Ark door, and managed to squeeze through. But its tail was caught in the door and was left behind in the Flood.

A Manx cat totally with a tail is called a *rumpy*. One with a little stub of a tail is a *stumpy*. Is a fat one a *dumpy*, an unfashionable one a *frumpy*, one with bad posture a *slumpy*, one with bad temper a *grumpy*, one with an attractive bod a *humpy*, one with acne a *bumpy*, one with fat feet a *clumpy*, one with frayed nerves a *jumpy*, one in a tight sweater a *lumpy*, one with a swollen face a *mumpy* and so on?

MANX CAT AND KITTENS.

How did the Manx cat lose its tail? It was bitten off on the Ark by its ancient enemy the dog.

According to legend, the Manx cat did not originate on the Isle of Man, situated between Great Britain and Ireland, but was brought there by Phoenician traders, who are reputed to have spread cats, like butter, over all the ports of the Old World.

According to another story, the Manx cat did not originate on the Isle of Man, but a tailless tom swam ashore from a gunboat of the Spanish Armada that was driven onto a rock, and fathered all future generations of Manx cats.

Although the cat population of the United States (34 million) is the largest in the world, it must seem to visitors to Rome, Italy, as though every cat in the world is loose in the piazzas of Roma. In fact, there are some 250,000 homeless cats in the city of Rome, 20,000 of them in the center, the largest stray cat population on record. They hang out at the Theater of Marcellus, the Colosseum, the Forum, the Pantheon, and many other places of tourist interest, and have become something of a tourist attraction themselves. The cats are gentle, happy and well-fed; the women of Rome see to that. Ten years ago, there were more than one hundred *gattare* ("cat ladies") in the center of the city alone, but, alas, their numbers have been dwindling, and with them the numbers of the cats as well. The center of Rome has been changing, and as more and more people move out of it to the suburbs, the cat ladies and the cats move, too. Now there are fewer than twenty *gattare,* and the ancient communities of roamin' Roman cats are gradually becoming smaller. Cats are time-honored denizens of Rome. Some say the first arrivals came with the Phoenicians. Imported to Rome from Egypt around 150 B.C., cats quickly changed from a luxury item to a necessity, as they protected the city's grain supplies and kept the rats and mice at bay. Encouraged to breed, they soon flourished. As Romans assimilated some forms of the Egyptian religion, cats became revered, and colonies of them resided near temples. An ancient regulation forbids the seizure of cats in Rome, and Mussolini, who was himself a cat lover, protected them from disturbance on the grounds that all national monuments were state property, including the *gatti,* and were under state protection. Since cats have been respected citizens of Rome for more than two thousand years, it seems likely that they will continue so in the millennia to come.

★ ★ ★ ★ ★ ★ ★ **SEEING STARS** ★ ★ ★ ★ ★ ★ ★

The Patsy Awards are the animal answer to the Oscars. Presented by the American Humane Association, they are annual awards for the best animal performance in a film. Five awards have been taken by cats; and one cat, Orangey, has won two Patsys, to make him the Kate Hepburn of the feline race. And now, the envelope, please.

> 1952—Rhubarb, in the film *Rhubarb* (Orangey).
> 1959—Pyewacket, the Siamese in *Bell, Book and Candle.*
> 1962—Cat, in *Breakfast at Tiffany's* (that's Orangey again).
> 1966—Syn, another Siamese, in *That Darn Cat.*
> 1975—Tonto, in *Harry and Tonto.*

A Poet's Cat, sedate and grave
As poet well could wish to have . . .
— William Cowper

About the poet Baudelaire, Champfleury quotes nineteenth century press reports from Paris: "It has become the fashion in the society formed by Baudelaire and his companions to make too much of cats, after the example of Hoffman, Edgar Poe and Gautier. Baudelaire, going for the first time to a house, and on business, is uneasy and restless until he has seen the household cat. But when he sees it, he takes it up, kisses and strokes it, and is so completely occupied with it that he makes no answer to anything that is said to him; he is a thousand miles away with his cat. People stare at this breach of good manners, but he is a man of letters, an oddity, and the lady of the house henceforth regards him with curiosity. The poet's turn is served. Let us only astonish the world at any price!" There are several poems in Baudelaire's *Fleurs du Mal* that deal with cats.

The French writer Colette, author of *Gigi* and the *Claudine* novels, was a celebrated cat lover, and cats figured in many of her books. The story is told that, on a visit to New York, with the usual celebrity hustle and bustle claiming her time and energies, she was returning to her Manhattan hotel one night when she spied a cat sitting in the street. At once she went over to talk to it, and the two of them mewed at each other for a friendly minute. Colette turned to her companion and said, with a heartfelt smile, *"Enfin! Quelqu'un qui parle francais!"* ("Finally! Someone who speaks French!")

The English philosopher Jeremy Bentham had a cat whom he fed macaroni at his table. He "knighted" the cat Sir John Langbourne. When Sir John was a young tom in his prime he was frisky and adventurous, and was wont to invite lady cats to share the garden of Bentham's home in Queen Square Place. As he grew older, Sir John became sedate, and Bentham retitled him the Reverend John Langbourne, and, when the cat was truly venerable, the Reverend Doctor John Langbourne.

HOW TO GET RID OF KITTENS

My next-door neighbors own a cat who cannot be spayed, because she moves too fast. She is either in heat, pregnant, or nursing, and they can never get her to the vet in time to stop the cycle. Out of necessity, they have developed the perfect method for getting rid of Fecundia's kittens.

As soon as the kittens are old enough to wean, my friends send out invitations to a cocktail party. Then they lay in a large supply of very cheap and potent gin, and absolutely no food. On the evening of the party, they put the kittens in the bathtub and shut the bathroom door. As each guest arrives, he is handed a "martini," which is a jelly glass full of gin with a twist. In fifteen minutes, most of the revelers have survived lift-off, and are on an earth-to-Mars course. Very soon the first of them has to go to the bathroom. He opens the door. He sees the bathtub filled with adorable kittens, tumbling over one another and squealing as they slide around on the slippery porcelain. They scrabble to get out, only to fall back again. Seen through a fog of cheap gin, it's an enchanting sight, sweet enough to melt the heart of a garage mechanic.

"Awwwwww," says the first guest, scooping out a favorite and cuddling it.

"Awwww," say the procession of tipsy guests, as all the kittens are tucked into overcoat pockets and carried home in a mushy haze of inebriated affection.

Then my friends take their phone off the hook and leave for the Caribbean, staying long enough to make sure that nobody would dare return a kitten.

It's an expensive method, and one requiring a large number of hard-drinking friends, but it never fails.

Fecundia is pregnant again, and my neighbors are thinking of moving away without telling the cat.

GEE WHIZ! BUT I'M LONESOME

How does a cat find its way back home over hundreds and even thousands of miles? What is the sense that leads an abandoned cat to follow its master to a new home it has never been to before? Documented cases of both phenomena abound, such as the case of a veterinarian who moved from New York to California, a distance of three thousand miles. He left his pet cat in New York, in a new home, but the cat turned up at his California front door three months later. Researchers call this "psi-trailing" — cats tracing their masters even to places they have never seen and which they inexplicably find. Drs. Karlis Osis and E. B. Forster and Prof. J. B. Rhine, all of the Duke University Laboratory of Parapsychology, have been studying this phenomenon of cat clairvoyance. Also examining the unexplained bump of direction in the cat are Prof. H. Precht and Dr. Elke Lindenlaub of Wilhelmshaven, Germany. They took cats on confusing drives around the city, to throw off the cats' sense of direction, and then to the lab, where the cats were placed in a large maze with twenty-four exits facing in all directions. In the overwhelming majority of cases, the cat would select the one exit out of the two dozen that lay most nearly in the direction of its home.

A man named Quick had a cat who broke its leg, and it was decided to do away with the cat. It was put into a sack and sent over Michipicoten Falls in Canada, a 123-foot drop. Quick and others watched the sack go over and be carried away by the swirling waters. When the bereaved arrived home, the cat was sitting on his front porch.

In 1979, a Siamese female named Sherry, belonging to Sgt. Guy Jones and his wife, escaped from her cage in the hold of a Pan Am jet between Guam and San Francisco as she was being flown to Jones' new military base. Nobody could find her for thirty-two days, but she did turn up, thinner and with her right back leg injured, but basically okay, on the thirty-third day. Pan Am officials estimated that Sherry had traveled 225,000 miles, to twelve countries, in a little over a month. When applied to for a statement, Sherry declined to comment, but her demeanor indicated that getting there was *not* half the fun.

Sometimes the homing instinct of the cat takes her *away* from her owners and back to her old haunts, as in the case of a cat named Thrum, who in 1964 was taken from Seminole, Oklahoma, to St. Louis, Missouri, a distance of 450 miles. Thrum left, and six weeks later turned up on her old doorstep in Seminole.

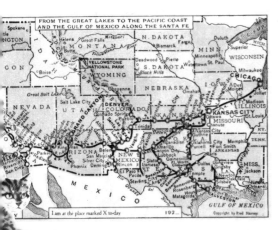

Tiger Frommelt, a male cat belonging to Tim and Susan Frommelt, was lost when the family was vacationing in Wasau, Wisconsin, in the summer of 1977. In February of 1978, Tiger turned up home in Dubuque, Iowa, having made a journey of 250 miles. Far from being ragged and starving, Tiger had put on weight.

More recently, a cat called Kittycat was a kitten in the family of Governor David Cargo of New Mexico. In 1971, the Cargo family moved out of the governor's mansion, and the new administration, Governor Bruce King and family, moved in. Kittycat went, of course, with the Cargos, but she soon deserted them and moved in with the Kings, to be closer to the mousehole of power. Upon the expiration of Governor King's four-year term, the King family moved to a ranch a fur piece from the state capitol, taking Kittycat with them. But she seemed to be pining for the fleshpots of Albuquerque, and hit the road again. She never made it, but returned disgruntled and settled into ranch life. Four years passed, and ex-Governor King ran for the office again, and won. Back they all went to the Governor's mansion again, Kittycat in the lead. It was her third term in office, one more than any governor of New Mexico has ever had.

In their #1 bestseller, *The Book of Lists,* David Wallechinsky, Irving Wallace, and Amy Wallace tell the astonishing story of Daisy, a cat picked up and adopted by a family on summer vacation in upstate New York. At the end of the summer, they chucked Daisy out again, but she was a cat not to be chucked lightly. Not only did she turn up on the doorstep of their New York City home a month later (a place she'd never seen before), but she was carrying a kitten in her mouth. She deposited the kitten and went back north for another one, then another one, and so on until she'd made a total of four trips back to her old home, each time bringing back one more kitten until there were five! That has to be a record of some kind, but we're not sure what.

The People's Almanac #2, by David Wallechinsky and Irving Wallace, reports the case of a pet cat who was given by an Oklahoma family to friends in California, and who made the 1,400-mile journey back to Oklahoma in an exhausting fourteen months. The prodigal cat was positively identified by its former family through an old hipbone deformity it suffered from.

I'm So Lonesome

A family that moved from Newnan, Georgia, to Spartanburg, North Carolina, owned a cat. It disappeared before they left Newnan, but turned up at their door in Spartanburg a year later.

THE LIBERATED CAT

Mark Twain said: "Of all God's creatures there is only one that cannot be made the slave of the lash. That one is the cat."

The independent cat, which comes and goes as it pleases, was the symbol of liberty among the ancient Romans. The goddess of liberty was depicted as holding a cup in one hand and a broken scepter in the other, a cat lying at her feet.

The cat was a symbol of independence to the Dutch, who used it on their banners in their struggle with Spain. The cat was also a symbol of liberty for the French during the French Revolution of 1789.

Siamese warriors used to train cats to sit upon their shoulders and utter warning cries if the enemy approached from behind.

In the 1930s a cat aided in the building of the Grand Coulee Dam by crawling through the winding pipeline with a string tied to its tail. The string was fastened to a rope, and the rope to the cable that the engineers had been unable to thread through the pipe.

Minnie Esso, chief mouser for the Standard Oil Development Co. of Bayonne, New Jersey, died in 1946. She had been on the payroll since 1933, fed on salmon and milk, and earning $4.40 a month. The president of the Standard Oil Company of New Jersey had personally dealt with matters of Minnie's coverage and other employee benefits under the company's annuity plan, which was just as well, since Minnie had mothered more than one hundred kittens. Minnie's position as chief mouser descended to her ten-month-old son, Timmie Esso.

Frederick the Great made cats the guards of army food supplies, and demanded of the towns he conquered that they supply him with cats for this purpose.

SEE THE CATS-KILL MOUNTAINS

The Magic Center on New York City's Eighth Avenue boasts a cat named Eggbag, named after a trick in which an egg is made to appear in a felt purse. Shop owner Russ Delmar has taught Eggbag to do a card trick. "Pick a card, any card," says Delmar to a shop visitor, who picks one, notes it, and replaces it in the deck. Delmar fans the deck for Eggbag, who pulls the right card out with his teeth. It is said that Eggbag is also working on the sawing-a-mouse-in-half trick, and the Houdini escape from pawcuffs.

In 1954, two cats made a test parachute jump from an altitude of 350 feet, in preparation for being air-lifted to a mouse-plagued British fort in the Malayan jungle. The garrison had sent an urgent call for relief from rodents destroying the food supply, and the cats were to be parachuted in by the RAF. The cats, chosen for their "reputations as go-getters," were described by an air-dispatch officer as "quite jolly about the whole thing. One is an off-white, the other a speckled sort of dun."

Possibly the most celebrated working cat in Great Britain was Peter, the Whitehall mouser. An out-of-work drifter, Peter entered Government service in 1948 as the only 007 (licensed to kill) on the Home Office payroll. Around his neck on a ribbon was an identity tag: "Peter, Home Office, S.W.1." He killed hundreds of rats for his keep, and earned 2s 6d, half-a-crown (then the equivalent of 50 cents) a week from the Treasury. In 1958, R. A. Butler, then Home Secretary, put Peter's picture on his Christmas card, and the cat enjoyed a brief moment of celebrity, becoming a minor TV figure. In his old age, Peter developed liver trouble and had to be put to sleep. Two Home Office librarians and a shetland pony named Goldie were graveside mourners. Government workers chipped in £8 ($22.40) to buy him an oak-veneered coffin with brass handles. Peter is buried in People's Dispensary for Sick Animals cemetery in Ilford, next to the grave of Coco, a mouse.

Palmer Cox

During the first World War, 500,000 cats were drafted by the British to detect and give early warning of gas attacks.

The United States Army Tank Corps

In Sicily there is a belief that if a black cat lives with seven masters, it will drag the seventh down to hell with it when it dies.

In Westminster, England, they say that at night Westminster cats leave the city for disreputable dissipation in a country house, which is why they look so draggle-tailed and worn-out the next day.

Although cats are not mentioned at all in the Old Testament, the Talmud includes this spell for gaining the power to see demons: "Find and burn the placenta of the first litter of a black cat (which must have been from its mother's first litter), then beat it to a powder and rub it into the eyes."

Romans consider cats to have supernatural powers, including that of "the evil eye," and a cat staring at a Roman will cause the human to cross his fingers and clutch at the talismans around his neck to avert the cat's power.
Romans passing cats on the street will often nod for good luck.

The Japanese believe that you can cure spasms by placing a black cat on the belly of the sick person.

Among ancient Celtic peoples was the belief that if you trod on a cat's tail, a serpent would sting you.

A French peasant legend holds that, if you tie a black cat to a spot where five roads meet and then let it loose, it will lead you to buried treasure.

There is an old belief in Normandy that a tortoiseshell cat climbing a tree means an accidental death is near, and that a black cat crossing your path by moonlight means you'd die in an epidemic. In Germany, superstition has it that if a sick man sees two cats fighting his death is near. In ancient Ephesus, Artemidorus held that to dream of being scratched by a cat meant sickness and trouble. In Cornwall, folk magic claims you can cure a stye in your eye by stroking your eye, in the direction away from the nose, with the tail of a black cat, all the while saying, "I poke thee, I don't poke thee, I toke the queff that's under the 'ee. Oh, qualyway, oh, qualyway." The same belief elsewhere in England stipulates that the cat must be a male.

A French custom: At harvest time a cat is decked in ribbons and flowers and cornstalks, first at the start of the reaping and then at the end of the harvest. This is obviously a symbolic form of sacrifice to the goddess of the harvest, since the cat is so closely associated with fertility and fertility goddesses. In much earlier days, in Russia as well as France, a cat was actually sacrificed and buried in the fields before the grain was sowed, a continuation into Christian times of pagan beliefs.

In 1949, the mummified body of a cat, with the mummified body of a rat in its mouth, was found behind a wall in a house in London. They had been put there about two hundred years before, when the house was built, "to keep out the devil."

If the neighbor's cat comes around for a visit, and sits listening, it's a sure sign that your neighbor is gossiping about you, and that the cat will bring home tales.

There's an old Buddhist belief that when an advanced person dies his soul enters into the body of a cat, remaining there until the cat dies, when it enters heaven.

In North Africa, an ear of corn is hung behind the door for luck, and is considered twice as lucky if a cat nibbles at it.

A Welsh superstition: Those who feed cats well will have sun on their wedding day.

From France: A girl who treads upon the tail of a cat will take a year longer to find herself a husband.

If a cat sneezes in front of the bride on her wedding day, it will be a happy marriage.

I beseech you

The familiar sculptured figure of the "Hallowe'en Cat" — black, with an arched back and a thick tail — did not commonly appear in American folk art until the twentieth century because many folk artists were superstitious, and thought that by creating the figure of the witch's cat, they were in danger of summoning the cat itself.

It's not sunshine or moonshine in a cat's eyes that makes them glow in the dark, but the *tapetum lucidum* membrane that reflects light. The cat's slit pupil is very sensitive to ultraviolet light, which helps her to see in the dark. Because she was once a night-hunter, science until only recently held that cats could see only black and white, but now researchers acknowledge that cats can perceive and be conditioned to distinguish among a limited color palette, telling red and blue from each other and from white, although green, white, and yellow probably all look much the same to a cat, and red is perceived as dark gray.

An ancient folktale has it that a female cat gives birth seven times—the first litter is one kitten only, the second, two, the third, three, and so on until the seventh birth makes a total of twenty-eight kittens, a magic number. Thus, the cat is tied in with the twenty-eight day lunar month, and is therefore a goddess of the moon. Plutarch, passing this tale along with some skepticism (anybody owning a female cat can vouch for its lack of verity) remarked, "Though such things may appear to carry an air of fiction with them, yet it may be depended upon, that the pupils of her eyes seem to fill and grow larger upon the full of the moon, and to increase again, and diminish in their brightness on its waning."

From an old Chinese book: "Someone has said that the pupils of the cat's eye marks the time; at midnight, noon, sunrise, and sunset, it is like a thread; at four o'clock and ten o'clock morning and evening, it is round like a full moon; while at two o'clock and eight o'clock, morning and evening, it is elliptical like the kernel of a date."

In China, cats are considered good luck, and have been household pets at least since the beginning of the Christian Era. Chinese believed that the gleam in a cat's eyes at night could detect and repel evil spirits; and Chinese would keep at least one household cat collared and chained so that it wouldn't roam away at night when its protection was most needed. The Chinese also shared a common belief around the world, shared by the Africans among others, that one can tell time by looking at a cat's eyes—the pupil is wide in the morning, a narrow vertical slit at noon, and broader again in the later afternoon.

Herodotus also tells of the Egyptian belief that a cat holds the sun in its eyes at night, a reference to the glowing of a cat's eyes in the dark, and, since the moon also holds the light of the sun at night, the cat is also associated with the moon.

CATS AND DEITIES

How did the myth that a cat has nine lives arise? The numbers 3 and 9 are linked with felines; 9 is the trinity of trinities. In Egyptian belief, there were three groups of gods, nine gods each. Since the Egyptian gods cherished cats, the first of the three groups of nine gods, being the most important, may have given the cat her nine lives. Freya, the Norse goddess associated with cats, is also linked to the number 9—she had power over the nine worlds, also over the ninth world.

The cat goddess of Egypt, Bast (Bastet or Pasht—from which name it is said we get the word Puss) was associated in the ancient world with the Greek Artemis, as the cat is a hunter by nature, and also with Isis, the mother goddess, since the cat is a wonderful mother.

The Norse goddess of love and beauty, Frigga or Freya, was always drawn in a chariot by a pair of cats. Odur, the summer sun, is Freya's husband, and her brother, Freyer, is the sunshine, thus the cat through Freya is linked to the sun. Friday is named for Freya and Freyer; because she was the goddess of love, Friday was considered the best day to marry. Farmers would place a bowl of milk in the cornfields for Freya's cats, to assure a good harvest. With the advent of Christianity, the Freya cult was driven underground and its followers eventually came to be seen as witches, and cats came to be associated with witches.

Another Norse myth: The god Thor visited Jotunheim, the home of the ice giants, to seek King Utgard-Loki. To prove his strength, he was required to lift a huge cat, supposedly the pet of the giants' children. Thor tried it, and discovered that he could lift only one of the cat's paws off the ground. But the cat was in fact the great serpent of Midgard, which circles the earth, and the giants were astonished that Thor could lift even one paw. One explanation of this myth is that the Egyptian cat worship spread, together with other aspects of Egyptian religion, through Europe by means of the Roman legions that had occupied Egypt, and that the identification of the cat with the serpent is a later form of the battle between the cat and the serpent Apep which figures so largely in ancient Egyptian belief. The cat in repose is a circle, and the Midgard serpent also represents a circle, therefore cat and snake are two sides of the same coin.

The cat, in ancient Roman times, was associated with Venus, not only because of its amatory nature, but because the cat is traditionally associated with a female deity—Isis, Bast, Artemis, Freya, and others. Here are two cat-and-Venus myths:

A man prayed to Venus to grant him a wife as beautiful as a cat. Obligingly, the goddess changed a cat into a woman and gave her to him as his bride. On their wedding night, a mouse ran into the bridal chamber, and the girl leaped out of bed like lightning and began chasing it.

Venus turned a cat into a beautiful woman and named her *Aileuros* (meaning "cat" in Greek). Aileuros, forgetting her origins, vied with the goddess herself in beauty and Venus, furious, changed her back into a cat.

SERIE 14 Nº 5   NEUE PHOTOGR. GESELLSCH. A.-G. STEGLITZ 1900

The Welsh prince Hywel Dda, or Howel the Good, died in A.D. 948. It was he who wrote the first Welsh codification of laws, embodying both the formal (royal) and customary (tribal) usages. The laws were codified according to regions, and here are the laws that governed cats:

From the Vendotian Code:

XI. The worth of a cat and her qualities is this:

1. The worth of a kitten from the night it is kittened until it shall open its eyes is a legal penny.
2. And from that time, until it shall kill mice, two legal pence.
3. And after it shall kill mice, four legal pence; and so it always remains.
4. Her qualities are to see, to hear, to kill mice, to have her claws entire, to rear and not devour her kittens, and if she be bought, and be deficient in any one of those qualities, let one-third of her worth be returned.

From the Dimetian Code:

XXXIII of Cats:

1. The worth of a cat that is killed or stolen: its head to be put downwards upon a clean even floor, with its tail lifted upwards, and thus suspended, whilst wheat is poured about it, until the top of its tail be covered; and that is to be its worth; if the corn cannot be had a milch sheep, with her lamb and her wool, is its value; if it be a cat that guards the King's barn.
2. The worth of a common cat is four legal pence.
3. Whoever shall sell a cat is to answer for her not going a-caterwauling every moon; and that she devour not her kittens; and that she have eyes, teeth, and nails; and being a good mouser.

From the Gwentian Code:

5. A pound is the worth of a pet animal of the king.
6. The pet animal of a *breyr* (one of the different types of freemen) is six score pence in value.
7. The pet animal of a *taeog* (a husbandman in liege of the King) is a curt penny in value.
53. There are three animals whose tails, eyes, and lives are of the same worth: a calf; a filly for common worth; and a cat; excepting the cat that shall watch the King's barn.

In the morning of the world, God called all the animals together to divide among them the attributes they would need in life. The beasts crowded around Him, clamoring their wants—speed, strength, intelligence, beauty, courage—and only the cat remained apart, silent. She asked for nothing, but sat and watched, and when she saw the scorpion raise his tail and go to sting the foot of God, the cat pounced, seizing him in her paws and knocking him senseless. God saw this, and gave freely to the cat everything the others were demanding. And that is why the scorpion lives his life in the dust, and why the cat smiles in her sleep.

When God made the world, He chose to put animals in it, and decided to give each whatever it wanted. All the animals formed a long line before His throne, and the cat quietly went to the end of the line. To the elephant and the bear He gave strength, to the rabbit and the deer, swiftness; to the owl, the ability to see at night, to the birds and the butterflies, great beauty; to the fox, cunning; to the monkey, intelligence; to the dog, loyalty; to the lion, courage; to the otter, playfulness. And all these were things the animals begged of God. At last He came to the end of the line, and there sat the little cat, waiting patiently.

"What will *you* have?" God asked the cat.

The cat shrugged modestly. "Oh, whatever scraps you have left over. I don't mind."

"But I'm God. I have *everything* left over."

"Then I'll have a little of everything, please."

And God gave a great shout of laughter at the cleverness of this small animal, and gave the cat everything she asked for, adding grace and elegance and, only for her, a gentle purr that would always attract humans and assure her a warm and comfortable home.

But he took away her false modesty.

CATS IN THE NEWS

John Kenneth Galbraith, who was United States Ambassador to India in 1963, became the center of a furor in the Pakistani National Assembly when he named his Siamese cat Ahmed. Since "Ahmed" is one of the forms of the name "Mohammed," Abbas Ali of the Islamic Democratic Group accused Ambassador Galbraith of a "deliberate insult" to Mohammed, and announced that the ambassador had offended the religious sentiments of Moslems everywhere. Ali demanded that the Pakistan government take immediate steps and that the National Assembly put aside its scheduled business to debate the matter. Khan Sabour, the leader of the government party, called the situation "very distressing," and promised the government would look into it. The Deputy Speaker, Afzal Cheema, conceded that the matter was indeed serious, and, if Ali's allegation was true, it was "much more serious than American arms aid to India." Meanwhile, in New Delhi, a United States Embassy spokesman issued a statement declaring that the cat was not named Ahmed at all, but rather Ahmedabad ("Ahmed's Place") after the capital city of the state of Gujarat, where the cat was presented to Ambassador Galbraith's children as a gift on a formal visit there in 1962. The Galbraith children decided that the cat should not, however innocently, become a cause for controversy, and they renamed it Gujarat.

A Mrs. Constance Martin, seventy, a British resident of Shanghai, was arrested by Chinese officials and urged by her friends to leave China, but was unwilling to desert her seventeen pet cats.

In 1970 the government of Colombia reported a critical shortage of cats, resulting in a dramatic increase in the rodent population and posing a serious threat to the agricultural economy of that South American state. Many Colombians were exposed to rat-bite and rat-carried infectious diseases, and even in upland Bogotá a cat had escalated in value and cost twelve dollars, the earnings of a manual worker for a six-day week. The reason behind the population decline of cats was thought to be man's use of insecticides and other poisons, which had entered the cat's food chain. The government took steps to conserve the cat population, and planned the importation of large numbers of cats.

The closing of the Brooklyn Navy Yard in June 1966 brought the threat of extinction to the 1,500 cats living in the Navy Yard buildings. It was feared that they would starve or thirst to death once the buildings had been sealed. Meanwhile, Brooklyn residents nearby feared an explosion of the rat population, held in check by the diligent Navy Yard cats. Mrs. Judith Scofield, president of the Save-A-Cat League, sent beseeching telegrams to President Lyndon Johnson, Senator Robert Kennedy and New York Mayor John Lindsay asking for help, since the league was unable to shelter the 1,500 cats, who had come ashore over the years from various ships, or were stray Brooklyn natives attracted to the Navy Yard by the available rats. In July, the Navy promised to take care of all cats left homeless by the closing of the Yard. A Navy official wrote to New York's Senator Jacob Javits, assuring him that the cat population was closer to 250 than 1,500, and that 200 of these had already been "relocated" to foster homes. The official promised that the remaining 50 would be fed regularly and left in the Yard to combat rats.

In 1978, the basement of the United Nations building in New York was discovered to be "infested" with cats, which the UN maintenance staff had been trying to trap and kill. An internal group calling itself the UN Animal Rights Club began lobbying in defense of the cats, but the UN's Management Service Chief, Henry Jaran, refused to return its calls. The cats had been soiling laundry, stores, and documents. Having gained recognition by the UN as an internal club, the Animal Rights people were authorized to confront Jaran, and a provisional agreement was struck, pending advice from the A.S.P.C.A., that whenever a cat was trapped, Jaran would call in the Animal Rights Club. This would appear to be rescue-by-committee, or par for the course at the UN, where nothing comes easy or without endless debate.

New Yorkers discovered that a mated pair of cats had been living on the tracks of the Times Square–to–Grand Central Station shuttle train. Their home was Track 3, under Times Square, five yards from where the train — which the cats ignore — comes to a halt before returning in the other direction. Cat-loving shuttle regulars brought them food wrapped in wax paper and aluminum foil; one could see salami sandwiches, cat food, table scraps, and water in plastic containers laid out on the platform near the cats' abode. Evidently the cats took little outings for fresh air in Times Square. When the female produced a litter of kittens, the mother nursed them right on the tracks until some-one took them away and found them a home, reportedly "in the country, on Long Island."

There is a prevailing myth that a cat cannot be out-stared by a human. That's puppy-poop. I personally have never known a cat who, once it discovered it was being stared at, did not suddenly remember a pressing engagement elsewhere.

People who do not care for cats are often heard to characterize them, in a stringent tone of voice, as "too damn independent." But, as Mary Abigail Dodge wrote, "What's virtue in a man can't be vice in a cat."

Webster's Third New International Dictionary defines "a clowder of cats" as a group of cats and adds that the word "clowder" comes from the word "clutter." But anybody who lives with cats knows that dogs clutter, cats tidy.

Catgut, we are happy to say, is made not of cats' intestines, but of those of sheep. The term "catgut" originated in Italy, where the original manufacturer, wishing to keep his formula a secret, deliberately misnamed his chief ingredient to throw the competition off the scent.

A Buddhist foundation, Jikeiin, operates a cemetery in Tokyo that will cremate your cat or dog on its death. For ten dollars a year, the pet's ashes are preserved until your own death, when you and your cat are interred together forever in Tama Dog and Cat Memorial Park (the bill for which is a prepaid $3,350).

In 1962, *Life* magazine reported that the keepers of the Albert Premier Shelter on Mont Blanc (8,875 feet) owned a kitten named Zizou, only four months old, who liked to climb mountains. Zizou could climb two thousand feet higher on his own, but sometimes reached even greater heights by hitching a ride in hikers' backpacks.

The Ralston Purina cat personality contest draws over a million entrants annually.

If God did not intend the cat to live happily with humankind, why is there a meow in the middle of the word "hoMEOWner"?

California, sunny home of nuts and berries, offers the following services for cats: acupuncturists, a cat resort, a cat department store, a feline rest home, a rent-a-cat agency, a pussycat dating service, cat psychics, cat psychiatrists, feline acting coaches, and an annual meowing contest.

The Axiom Market Research Bureau, Inc., reports: cat owners like *Time,* nonowners prefer *Newsweek*. Don't ask us why.

The last known descendant of Samuel Pepys's cat died in 1933. This was Brutus, the cat belonging to the London National Gallery of Art.

The simple little game of cat's-cradle, played with string, is known the world over. Its possible origin was in a solar rite. In hot countries the "cradle" was designed to lure the cat, who is everywhere associated with the sun, to its rest in order to give humans respite from the heat. In the cold countries it is designed to trap the cat and delay the sun's departure.

A deaf taxpayer, living alone except for his cat, claims his cat as a deduction on the grounds that the cat alerts him to possible dangers by its reaction to unusual sounds. The cat is registered as a "hearing aid." The IRS ruled (1980) that the cost of maintaining this cat is deductible, but that its decision applies to this taxpayer alone, and cannot be cited as precedent by other cat owners making similar claims, which would have to be examined on their own merits.

The word "tabby" may come from the Turkish name "Attabiya," the quarter of Baghdad where watered silk was manufactured in the twelfth century. The cat's stripes are like the moiré pattern of the fabric. Although the cat is the only domestic animal not mentioned in the Bible, remains of cats, possibly domesticated, were found in the excavation of Jericho (from the 6,700 B.C. stratum).

Japanese keep statues of cats by their front doors and in their restaurants, not only for good luck, but to ward off rodents.

In ancient China, dead cats were not buried but hung on trees.

From *The New York Times,* November 11, 1942, reprinted in its entirety (dateline, French Lick Springs, Indiana): "All black cats in this municipality will wear bells on Friday, the 13th, by municipal decree, as a war measure to alleviate mental strain on the populace. The practice was introduced on Friday, Oct. 13, 1939, and enforced on all fateful Fridays since, except last year, when a number of minor mishaps occurred."

The Isle of Man issued currency in 1971 for the first time in 130 years, crown coins. On the head of the coin, Queen Elizabeth II; on the reverse, a Manx cat.

In the Hindu religion, the housing and feeding of one cat is theoretically demanded of all the faithful, and the prophet Mohammed himself is widely believed to have cut off the sleeve of his robe rather than disturb the sleep of his pet cat Muezza, which was curled up on it. The name Muezza means "fairest and gentlest."

Dr. B. L. Mosely, pathologist at the University of Missouri and associate professor of veterinary pathology, believes that the old wives' tale that cats lick themselves before a storm may be true. Prior to an electrical storm, the air is charged with static electricity, causing cats' fur to attract dust particles if the fur is dry. So the cat grooms itself to dampen and clean its fur.

KITTENS FOR SALE:

2 DAYS OLD
5 " "
9 " "
17 " "
Free Cats

In Scotland, a male cat is called a "gib," and the female a "doe."

A classified ad in the Orleans, Massachusetts, *Oracle*, 1966: "Cats for rent. A few choice solids and popular patterns still available. Don't be without a pet on your vacation. 25¢ first week, 10¢ a week thereafter. The Oldest Cat Rental Agency on Cape Cod. . . ." When interviewed by *Sports Illustrated*, the agency owners (their agency was then two weeks old), a young couple, said, "We have eight cats, and we don't need eight cats. Two or three are fine." The eight cats included a number of kittens; the "agency" was fearful of selling or giving away the kittens to vacationers, lest they be abandoned at the end of the holiday, but hoped that, if the "renter" liked the cat or kitten, he might want to take it home with him. "Our first customer is coming this afternoon," confided the couple to the reporter. "A man called and wants a calico for two weeks. He has field mice."

When boats are about to leave harbor, they whistle — half an hour before departure, the whistle is to summon the crew; the fifteen-minute whistle is to call stragglers; the five-minute whistle is called "cat's whistle."

There is a Mohammedan tradition that says: "When Noah took into the Ark a pair of each of the animals, a male and a female, his followers said to him, 'How are we and our cattle to live in peace and security while the lion is with us?' God therefore caused the lion to be seized and overpowered with fever (and that was the first occasion on which fever visited the earth) and that is why the lion is always in a state of fever. They next complained of the rat, which, they said, would spoil the food supplies and other goods on board. God therefore caused the lion to sneeze, and from the sneeze came forth the cat. The rat then hid itself from the cat, as it does to this day."

And here is a Moslem riddle: Why do cats close their eyes when drinking milk? Answer: So that when Allah asks if they'd had their milk, they can (in hope of being given more) truthfully say they haven't seen any.

 **NATURAL HISTORY**

With the exception of the domestic cat, which humans have carried to all parts of the globe, only one of the thirty-six species of cat is common to both the Old World and the New: the lynx, *Felis lynx.*

There are three or five genera of the cat family, depending on which naturalists you believe. The genus *Panthera* (sometimes called *Leo)* includes: the clouded leopard *(Panthera nebulosa)*, the leopard *(Panthera pardus)*, the lion *(Panthera leo,* or sometimes *Leo leo)*, the snow leopard *(Panthera uncia),* and the tiger *(Panthera tigris)*, all found in the Old World; and the jaguar *(Panthera onca)*, found in the New World. Among the five-genera naturalists, the snow leopard and the clouded leopard occupy individual genera, in which each reigns alone, and in which they are classified *Uncia uncia* and *Neofelis nebulosa* respectively.

The only cat in the genus *Acinonyx* is the Old World cheetah, *Acinonyx jubatus*. The cheetah is different in numerous ways from the other cats, among them its so-called inability to retract its claws (in fact, they are retractable) and the rather doglike shape of its head.

All the other cats, including Puss Sit-by-the-Fire *(Felis catus)* belong to the genus *Felis.* Here they are, from the Old World first: African golden cat *(Felis aurata)*, black-footed cat *(Felis nigripes)*, Bornean red cat *(Felis badia)*, caracal *(Felis caracal)*, Chinese desert cat *(Felis bieti)*, domestic cat *(Felis catus*—also in the New World), European wildcat *(Felis silvestris)*, fishing cat *(Felis viverrina)*, flat-headed cat *(Felis planiceps)*, jungle cat *(Felis chaus)*, Kaffir cat *(Felis libyca)*, leopard cat *(Felis bengalensis)*, the lynx *(Felis lynx*—also in the New World), marbled cat *(Felis marmorata)*, Pallas' cat *(Felis manu)*; rusty-spotted cat *(Felis rubiginosa)*, sand cat *(Felis margarita)*, serval *(Felis serval)*, Temminck's cat *(Felis temmincki)*. From the New World come the Andean cat *(Felis jacobita)*, bobcat *(Felis rufa)*, Geoffroy's cat *(Felis geoffroyi)*, jaguarundi *(Felis yagouarundi)*, kodkod *(Felis guigna)*, little spotted cat *(Felis tigrina)*, margay *(Felis wiedi)*, ocelot *(Felis pardalis)*, pampas cat *(Felis colocolo)*, puma or cougar *(Felis concolor)*.

Although the cat's purr is unique, nobody actually knows how she does it. The mechanism is still only guessed at, but there are two prevailing theories. First, because the purr is felt in the larynx area, it's believed that it's due to the vibrations of the two membranes behind the true vocal cords, called "the false vocal cords." The other theory suggests that the purr is due to an alteration in the turbulence of the blood, which sets up vibrations in the thorax that are passed up the windpipe to resonate in the sinus cavities and emerge as the purr.

CHRISTIANITY AND THE CAT

In the Dark Ages of early medieval Europe, after the collapse of the Roman Empire, literacy and scholarship were kept alive by the clergy, most particularly the Irish monks. This anonymous little poem written in Latin in the margins of an eighth- or ninth-century manuscript of the Codex of St. Paul, found in the Irish monastery of Carinthia, celebrates both the joy of learning and the joy of owning a cat, comparing the skills used by both monk and cat. It is a thorough delight, and it also explains why so many Irish cats, especially white ones, are even today named Pangur Ban (White Pangur).

Here it is, in part:

> I and Pangur Ban, my cat,
> 'Tis a like task we are at;
> Hunting mice is his delight,
> Hunting words I sit all night.
>
> Oftentimes a mouse will stray
> In the hero Pangur's way;
> Oftentimes my keen thought set
> Takes a meaning in its net.
>
> When a mouse darts from its den,
> O how glad is Pangur then!
> O what gladness do I prove
> When I solve the doubts I love!
>
> So in peace our tasks we ply,
> Pangur Ban, my cat and I;
> In our arts we find our bliss,
> I have mine and he has his.
>
> Practice every day has made
> Pangur perfect in his trade;
> I get wisdom day and night
> Turning darkness into light.
> — Translated by Robin Flower

There is a legend that, as Mary was giving birth to Jesus in the stable, a cat lay there giving birth to a litter of kittens. This seems to arise less from Christian belief than from the long association of the cat with fertility in pre-Christian times. Another legend explains why the cat wears an "M" on its forehead. As Mary held the newborn infant Jesus in her arms, the cat, curious as always, came up to see the baby, and stuck its face too close for the Virgin's liking. She placed a gentle hand on its brow and pushed its face away; where her fingers touched, an "M" for "Mary" was left behind, which the cat wears to this very day.

St. Gertrude of Nivelles is the patron saint of travelers, gardeners, and cats. It is she who is invoked by those plagued by mice.

St. Yves of Treguier, Brittany, is the patron saint of lawyers. He is often depicted either with a cat or as a cat himself, because lawyers are said to play with their victims in court as cats play with captured mice.

At the end of the nineteenth century, there was a "cat cloister" next to the church of San Lorenzo in Florence, Italy. Inside the courtyard of the cloister was an "island" that was home to many stray cats. It offered free access to homeless felines, and a legacy, provided by a Florentine, fed them.

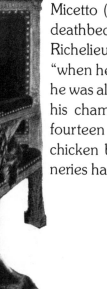

Christianity has brought to the feline race a series of ups and downs. Many prominent religious figures were felinophiles—among them the saints Francis, Martha, Jerome, Patrick, Agatha, and Gertrude of Nivelles. Of Pope Gregory the Great it was written that "he liked stroking his cat better than anything"; Cardinal Wolsey, Henry VIII's minister, took his cat with him to state functions, inspiring one foreign diplomat to write in a letter home that nothing like it had been seen since Caligula made his horse a Senator of Rome. Pope Leo XII gave his beloved tabby Micetto (it lived in a fold in his robe) to his best friend on his deathbed. It was written of the seventeenth century Cardinal Richelieu that his passion for his cats was so close to fanatic that "when he rose in the morning and when he went to bed at night he was always surrounded by a dozen of them. . . . He had one of his chambers fitted up as a cattery." The Richelieu cats—all fourteen of them—were waited upon by servants and fed on chicken breasts cooked into a pâtè. In the Middle Ages, nunneries had a rule: "Ye, my sisters, shall have no beast but a cat."

 Yet, it was Christianity that brought the cat to its darkest hour. In combating the pagan elements of religion, which went underground with the advent of Christianity and reemerged as witchcraft, the Church placed a stigma on the innocent cat because of its affiliations with the older gods, now deemed witches. Cats became "familiars," and were horribly persecuted—roasted alive, flayed, disemboweled, and tortured in hundreds of fiendish ways. The culmination of centuries of cat persecution came when the cat was denounced officially in 1348 by Pope Innocent VIII, who demanded in his papal bull "Against Sorcery" the death of cats and all those who harbored them. Thousands of cat lovers and millions of cats died during the Middle Ages because of the Church's insistence that the animal was evil. So many cats were killed, in fact, that the rat population increased mightily, leading to the great bubonic plague, or Black Death, in 1348, which decimated Europe. A bitter irony, but during the plague, a cat was worth its weight in gold.

GOOD ADVICE

Many cats eat plants, and you should keep a pot of something green, like catnip or sedum, for your cats to chew on. What they *shouldn't* chew on is listed below, for your information and their protection.

Houseplants poisonous or dangerous to cats

philodendron
poinsettia
oleander
  (usually fatal)
rhododendron
holly
lantana
pine needles

dumb cane
  (Diefenbachia)
Jerusalem cherry
snow-on-the-
  mountain
hydrangea
sheep laurel
azalea

elephant ear
  (caladium)
crown of thorns
laurel
bittersweet
mistletoe
English ivy

Garden plants poisonous or dangerous to cats

boxwood   privet   daphne
andromeda   monkshood   foxglove
lily-of-the-valley

Also, flower bulbs such as narcissus, daffodil, hyacinth, and amaryllis will upset a cat's digestion but will probably do no serious damage.

Plants that cats seem to love the scent of

leeks   asparagus   pinks
eucalyptus   mint   mimosa
lavender   catnip   catmint
carnation   oleander   cat thyme
papyrus   (beware!)
silver vine   valerian
     tuberoses

THE LEGEND OF THE BURMESE CAT

In 1898, the *kittahs* or priests of the Temple of Lao-Tsun, Burma, presented an Englishman, Russell Gordon, with a plaque showing the Sacred Cat at the feet of a bizarre deity whose eyes were made of sapphires. There were a hundred temple cats present, kept as sacred oracles. The priests told Gordon this story of the origin of these cats:

Many hundreds of years ago an old *kittah* named Mun-Ha, "the most precious among the precious, for whom the god Song-Hio had woven the beard of gold," lived in the temple with his white oracle cat, Sinh, "whom the *kittahs* fervently revered." The cat's eyes were a golden yellow, and they contemplated the goddess, whose eyes were sapphires. One night, at moonrise, "the barbarian Thais" threatened the temple, and the old *kittah* Mun-Ha died, in the presence of the goddess and his cat. Sinh leaped onto the holy throne, climbed on his dead master's head, and a miraculous transformation took place. As the cat faced the goddess, his white fur turned a golden yellow, and his golden eyes changed to the color of the goddess's sapphires. His four brown paws, which were touching the holy skull, turned pure white. The transformed cat turned toward the South Door of the Temple and kept his gaze steadfast. So compelling was his stare that the other priests felt new vigor, and they repelled the invader. Sinh remained fixed in the same position for seven days and six nights, staring intently at the goddess and refusing all nourishment. On the seventh day he died, without ever having moved a muscle. The cat and the soul of the master ascended to heaven. Seven days after Sinh's death, the *kittahs* assembled before the goddess to choose a new high priest, successor to Mun-Ha. Suddenly, the one hundred temple cats came in.

Each and every one of them was now golden yellow, with white feet and sapphire-blue eyes. From then on, whenever one of the sacred cats dies, he takes a priest's soul up to heaven with him.

ANOTHER LEGEND

They say that Charles I of England had a black cat, which he carried with him everywhere he went, claiming that the cat was his luck. When the cat died, the king wailed, "My luck is gone." He was arrested the following day and later beheaded by Oliver Cromwell.

TEA TIME.

A contemptuous word for a nonalcoholic
beverage, particularly tea: cat-lap.

Here is an absolutely absurd story, yet apparently quite true: In
1877, a Belgian cat appreciation society proposed using cats in
place of carrier pigeons. They hauled thirty-seven unsuspecting
cats into the countryside some twenty miles from Liège and
turned them loose at 2:00 P.M. The first cat arrived home at 6:48
P.M. All the others, dusty, footsore, and no doubt out of sorts,
straggled in over the next twenty-four hours, proving that somewhere in their furry bosoms lay a homing instinct. So the society
voted to set up a cat courier service between Liège and the
surrounding villages. Fortunately for the cats, nothing came of it.
Would they have called it Wells Furgo?

When a Walloon girl wants to dismiss an
unwanted suitor, she gives him a cat and
orders him to go away and count its hairs.

Chess champion Alexander Alekhine took his pet cat with him to a chess tournament in Warsaw in 1935, and set it on his lap as he played. The steady gaze of the cat so disconcerted Alekhine's opponents that they demanded the pet's removal, and got it.

Confucius was a cat lover, and Mohammed is said to have preached while holding a cat in his arms. Cats were kept in the temples in Japan to guard the precious manuscripts against depredations by rodents.

Cats have scent glands on their heads and faces. When you stroke their heads, the glands leave a faint scent of them on your hands, and the cat enjoys the odor as much as the stroking. This is also why they bump you with their heads as a sign of affection, and why they "nose-kiss" other cats. They also have scent glands under the tail, on either side of the anus, which is why they're forever sniffing at one another's rear ends when they meet.

Persian cats, like Samoyed dogs, are believed to have descended from the steppe cats of Central Asia. They have long fur and small ears, as Samoyeds do, to protect them from the cold.

Cats groom their fur more in warm weather than in cold. The evaporation of saliva on the skin helps to cool the animal. Cats also wash during times of crisis—when they are frightened, puzzled, embarrassed. Their temperature rises (as man's does when he sweats or blushes with embarrassment) and the licking is an instinctive cooling down.

The reason cats bury their excrement is to keep the scent from reaching the nostrils of the smaller animals upon which it preys and the larger animals that prey upon it.

Contrary to popular belief, cats do not purr only when happy. They also purr when they are in great pain.

Polydactylism, or extra toes on the paws, is about seven times more prevalent in Boston than in New York. The mutation is therefore believed to have arrived in the port of Boston by sea, then spread very slowly by land. Port towns do tend to show a wide variety of cat mutations, because ships' cats go ashore to mate, just like sailors. On land, mutations spread very slowly, since cats stick closer to home.

Ponder this: in 1981, according to New York City's Department of Health, 12,565 dogs bit New Yorkers, but only 826 cats. Probably this statistic means little more than the fact that cats are finicky, and New Yorkers taste terrible.

Although a cat is only one-fifteenth the size of a human, there are more bones in the cat's body, 230 to a man's 206. Many of these bones are in the tail—the cat's, not the human's.

The first dirigible to cross the Atlantic from England to America left East Fortune, Scotland, on July 2, 1919, and landed in Mineola, New York, on July 6, commanded by Major G. H. Scott. Aboard were, among others, a kitten named Jazz and a stowaway named Ballantyne, whose ambition to become a pilot was later fulfilled.

When a cat drinks water it takes four or five laps for every time it actually swallows.

Like the mongoose, cats are not afraid of snakes and can kill them.

The Abyssinian cat has also been called the "rabbit cat" or "the bunny cat," because the fur is ticked—that is, each individual hair shows lighter and darker coloration.

Mimi Vang Olsen

For decades, it has been assumed that the allergy that causes some humans to sneeze, wheeze, choke, and weep in the presence of cats was not cat-fur itself, but the dander, a form of animal dandruff, on the animal's skin. But Dr. John L. Ohman, a Boston physician, who has worked for years on a serum to combat cat allergies, now believes otherwise. It appears that the villain of the piece is not the dander per se, but the saliva the cat deposits on its skin when it washes itself. "The saliva," states Dr. Ohman, "contains a large amount of the allergen that we've isolated that seems to be the major component causing the allergy."

Cats can sleep anytime, anywhere, under any circumstances, in any kind of weather, day or night. They sleep two-thirds of their lives away, twice as much as most other members of the animal kingdom.

Ripley's *Believe It or Not* says that the Burmese cat is the only breed possessing tear ducts and shedding tears. A Burmese was observed to cry when its cat companion died. But St. George Mivart, the cat anatomist, says that cats in general do have tear ducts.

In the ruins of the Roman city Pompeii, destroyed by a volcano eruption in 79 A.D., was found the skeleton of a woman with the skeleton of a cat curled in her arms. They died together.

A report by Lieutenant Colonel A. Buchanan, a British Army officer in nineteenth-century India, concerned itself with *Cats as Plague Preventers,* and pointed out that one village of forty houses that contained thirty-six cats suffered not one case of plague, while in a similar-size village with no cats at all, twenty-one cases of plague broke out.

The Associated Press reports that cats in Florida are leading a particularly hazardous existence because they catch so many lizards. If the cat eats a certain lizard's tail, which it often sheds in its effort to escape, the cat incurs the risk of going cross-eyed and losing its sense of balance and direction. This is due to the poison in the lizard's tail. One cat reportedly ate a tail and was cross-eyed for five months, when, upon eating a second lizard tail, her eyes straightened, but she lost her hearing. What we'd like to know is why on earth she went back for a second helping?

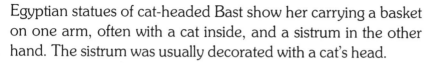

Egyptian hieroglyphics contain five pictographic symbols for the cat.

The Egyptian Mau cats currently bred in Great Britain have marks on their brows that resemble the scarab beetle, a sacred symbol of Ancient Egypt. Cat statuettes of the Middle Kingdom, the time of the great Pharaohs, also frequently bear the scarab on their foreheads. The modern Maus are bred to resemble as closely as possible the cats seen in ancient Egyptian wall paintings.

The word "Puss" has been said to come from the Egyptian name for the cat goddess, Pasht. But, in fact, it was first recorded in use in 1605, about two-hundred years before the Rosetta Stone was discovered that deciphered Egyptian hieroglyphics for the world and gave rise to Egyptology. "Puss" probably derives from the sound we all make when we see a beloved cat—the little calling word, Pssss, psss.

Egyptian statues of cat-headed Bast show her carrying a basket on one arm, often with a cat inside, and a sistrum in the other hand. The sistrum was usually decorated with a cat's head.

The Egyptian name for cat is (masculine) "mau," and (feminine) "mait." The Chinese name is "mao" or "miu," and these names are most probably based on the cat's meow. The Latin word "cattus" is likely derived from the Aryan "ghad," *to catch.*

Cats appeared in the early Pliocene period of geologic history, seven million years ago. The earliest record of domestication occurred around 1,500 B.C. in Egypt, but was probably earlier. The cat was worshipped as a sacred animal in Egypt as early as 2,500–2,200 B.C., but the cat may have still been in a wild state then. Wall tiles showing cats exist from ancient Crete (around 1,600 B.C.); the cat was certainly in Greece by the fifth century B.C., and it is referred to by Aristophanes and Menander, among other classical writers. The cat spread from Egypt to Babylonia and from there to India. It may have been known to the ancient Etruscans, but the evidence is doubtful. On the other hand, if the evidence is true, then the Etruscans might have been the first people in Europe to have domesticated the cat.

The very first pun recorded in history concerned a cat. It dates back to the second millennium before Christ, occurs in the Egyptian Book of the Dead, and reads something like this: The cat is called Mau by reason of the speech of the god Sa, who said, concerning him, "He is like unto that which he hath made." The pun lies in the fact that the word for cat and the word for like are both Mau; it loses something in the translation, granted, but no doubt it is hilarious to an ancient Egyptian.

Although the laws of Ancient Egypt forbade cats to be taken out of the country, and efforts were made to retrieve stolen cats and bring them back to Egypt, the domesticated cat did eventually make its way around the world. Because of its usefulness in keeping down the rats aboard ship, Phoenician sailors, who were the most courageous and far-sailing of men (they were the first to bring back tin from Britain with which to make bronze), managed to distribute them everywhere. By 900 B.C. cats were everywhere in Europe. Roman soldiers took them along, too, and introduced them to England when they conquered Britain. Remains of domestic cats were found in the ruins of the town of Silchester, Roman Britain, and little paw prints have been found in the tiles of Roman villas, much as children leave their footprints in wet cement. The earliest mention of the cat in India is around 100 B.C. Cats were introduced into Japan from China, where they appeared around 500 B.C. In China the cat was deified; peasants, who owed the safety of their grain to cats, worshipped the cat as the god Li-Shou. In eighteenth-century Japan, the temple of Gotokuji in Tokyo was consecrated to the cat, and effigies of cats are everywhere around it. Cats officially became Japanese citizens in A.D. 999, when a litter of kittens was born in the Imperial Palace at Kyoto, delighting the emperor. A tabby cat was said to have come over on the Mayflower, and, in 1749, the importation of cats to the Colonies was approved. The cat was brought to Canada by French missionaries, and it surprised the Indians greatly, being so different in size and nature from the native wild cats.

GREAT CAT QUOTATIONS

We cannot, of course, without becoming cats,
perfectly understand the cat-mind.
— Mivart

"If man could be crossed with the cat, it would improve man, but it
would deteriorate the cat."
— Mark Twain

"A house without a cat, and a well-fed, well-petted, and properly
revered cat, may be a proper house, perhaps, but how can it prove
its title?"
— Mark Twain

"Cats are a mysterious kind of folk. There is more passing in their
minds than we are aware of."
— Sir Walter Scott

"Cats and monkeys, monkeys and cats
— all human life is there."
— Henry James

GOOD-MORNING.

"The cat lives alone. He has no need of society. He obeys only when he wishes, he pretends to sleep the better to see, and scratches everything he can scratch."

—Chateaubriand

"When I play with my cat, who knows whether she is not amusing herself with me more than I with her?"

—Montaigne

"By associating with the cat, one only risks becoming richer. . . ."

—Colette

 **THE MAINE COON CAT**

Turkish sailors also brought their long-haired Angora cats to Maine, where they mated with the local pusses to produce the Maine coon cat. Because so many of these kittens had shaggy coats with raccoon-striped markings, the legend grew that the Maine coon cat was the result of a mating between a cat and a raccoon. This is not only false, but insulting. They are just good friends.

Another legend of the origin of the Maine coon cat has it that the breed are direct descendants of the cats of Marie Antoinette. The French queen, fearing for her life in the imminent revolution, planned her escape to the United States, sending her beloved cats on ahead of her. The cats lived and flourished, but the queen perished on the guillotine.

 **FEEBLE JOKES**

Two cats wander onto the sidelines of a tennis court and sit there watching the ball fly back and forth, back and forth.

First Cat: "The one in the blue shorts has a good forehand, but a weak backhand and a terrible serve."

Second Cat: "How do you know so much about tennis?"

First Cat: "My old man's in the racket."

Q: Where does a two-thousand pound gorilla sleep?
A: Anywhere it wants to.
Q: Where does a ten-pound cat sleep?
A: Anywhere it wants to.

 **A LEGEND**

God called the animals together and gave each his choice of the food he would eat on earth. When it came to the cat's turn, God said, "You can be fed by a fisherman, a hunter, or a farmer. Which do you choose?"
The cat replied, "I want to be fed by a lady who leaves the kitchen door open."
And thus it was ordained.

" The first thing I noticed was a craving for mice ! "

THE TALKING CAT

Anybody who has ever lived with a cat knows that the cat can talk. Sometimes with words, sometimes not. They can say, "Hello. How are you? I missed you." Or "Don't come around me looking for affection, after you've been gone three days. I don't even recognize you." Or "Kidney! How delightful!" or "Fried eggs! Yeccchhh!" Or "Have you a lap available?" Or "What does a cat have to do around here to get fed?" And a host of other useful phrases, including "Please" and "Thank you" and "Open the door, I want to get in (or out)." Scientists have long been fascinated by the mechanism of animal speech. In the eighteenth century, naturalist Dupont de Nemours made enormous efforts to understand and characterize the various mews, chirps, meows, trills, and howls that make up pussycat vocalization: "Its claws and the power of climbing trees which its claws give it, furnish the cat with resources of experience and ideas denied the dog. The cat, also, has the advantage of a language which has the same vowels as pronounced by the dog, and with six consonants in addition, *m, n, g, h, v,* and *f*. Consequently the cat has a greater number of words. These two causes, the finer structure of its paws, and the larger scope of oral language, endow the solitary cat with greater cunning and skill as a hunter than the dog."

Most of the words cats say are uttered with the mouth shut, and consist of consonants like *m* and *r*. When a cat "talks" to its owners, it uses vowels and makes specific demands using specific words. Cats have wide vocabularies, and at least sixteen different vocalizations have been recognized. Siamese are the most talkative breed in general, as are other Eastern varieties.

Our word for cat talk in English is "meow." In French it's *miauler;* in German, *miauen;* in Sanskrit, *madj, vid, bid;* in Greek, *larungizein;* in Chinese, *ming;* in Arabic, *naoua.*

Professor Alphonse Leon Grimaldi of Paris claims that he has learned cat "language," and says there are about six hundred words, and that the language itself bears a resemblance to modern Chinese.

THE PROVERBIAL PUSS

"What is born of a cat will catch mice." Meaning: You can dress yourself up and pass yourself off, but you can't change your basic nature.

The English say: "The cat shuts its eyes when it steals cream," referring to a person who is blind to his own faults.

Also from England: "Though the cat winks a while, yet sure she is not blind."

"When cat and mouse agree, the farmer has no chance."

"Better be the head of a cat than the tail of a lion."

"When the cat washes her face, company is coming."

A British saying: The cat has nine lives — three for playing, three for straying, three for staying.

A twelfth-century English proverb: "Wel wote hure cat whas berd he likat," or "The cat knows whose beard he licks."

From the Chinese: "A lame cat is better than a swift horse when rats infest the palace."

Here's a proverb: "They that ever mind the world to win/Must have a black cat, a howling dog, and a crowing hen."

From the Dutch: "A cat that meweth catcheth few mice." In other words, keep your mouth shut and take care of business.

From the Danish: "It takes a good many mice to kill a cat."

"A cat with a straw tail shouldn't sit with her back to the fire."

An English proverb: "To kiss a black cat will make one fat. To kiss a white cat will make one lean."

Proverbs such as "All cats are gray in the dark," "When the cat's away the mice will play," "Can the cat help it if the maid is a fool?" and "A cat in mittens catches no mice" are prevalent all over the world and exist in one form or another in a great many languages.

 **WITCHCRAFT**

The blackest hour in the history of the cat struck when the cat became wrongfully associated with the devil and his minions, the witches. Belief in witches followed the spread of Christianity. Mother and earth goddesses were forced underground, and the new religion took the place of the old. Cats had been associated with pagan goddesses such as Hecate, Queen of the Underworld, Freya, goddess of fertility, Isis, Artemis the nature goddess, and, as they became menacing instead of benevolent figures, the cat became "the familiar," the intermediary of the devil. Satan was believed to change himself into a cat; witches were known to take on cat forms, particularly those of black cats. Hecate, who became Queen of Hell in Christian superstition, could turn herself into a cat and did so frequently. The Dark Ages were dark indeed for the cat. Although the cat enjoyed renewed respect and was treated royally any time Europe was threatened by bubonic plague, which is carried by rats, in times of good health the cat was subject to hideous tortures and agonizing deaths by fire, water, hanging, and flaying. After the Papal Bull against sorcery issued by Pope Innocent in 1348, when it became a crime punishable by death to own or harbor a cat, cats died by the millions all over Christian Europe.

In fact, innocent cats were accepted by self-professed witches and wizards and used in black magic. Drawing a cat through the fire was believed to enable the witch to raise a storm at sea. When James I of England was returning home to Scotland from Denmark with his Danish bride, his ship encountered a mighty storm that nearly wrecked her, and James was convinced that witches were trying to take his life. A witchhunt ensued, and several "conspirators" were arrested. Chief among them was a Dr. John Fian, who had been seen to chase a cat in Tranent and be carried high above the ground, with great swiftness and as lightly as the cat itself, over a high dike. When put to the question, Fian confessed that he had chased the cat because Satan had commanded him to take cats and cast them into the sea to raise

the winds for destruction of ships and boats. His accomplice, Agnes Sampson, confessed under torture that she and two hundred other witches had set sail in sieves with their cats and had thrown the creatures overboard directly into the path of the king's ships, to raise a storm, and that only the King's steadfast faith in God had saved him from their satanic intentions.

It was also believed that the demon Bael had three heads, that of a man, a toad, and a cat. People believed that all cats had a pact with the devil; that they attended unholy witches' sabbaths; that they could speak in human tongues, that they guarded crossroads by night; that they drank human blood, and other unspeakable and destructive misconceptions.

In Salem, during the witchhunts of the seventeenth century, innocent, addled old women were accused of witchcraft, especially if they had cats by their firesides, and many were hanged. It wasn't until the Enlightenment spread over Europe, removing the last vestiges of benighted superstition from many (but not all) of the population, and ushering the world into the Age of Reason, that cats could begin to feel secure and enjoy once more the respect and affection of humans.

I call this story "The Cat's Revenge."

I once knew a fellow named Seth Stone, who was one of life's losers. Charming, affable, well-educated, intelligent, Stone possessed a will to succeed that was surpassed only by his will to fail. For every steak tartare he washed down with champagne at the Four Seasons, he spent a night of fasting and prayer at the Salvation Army. In one of his periods of famine, some Europe-bound friends asked him to cat-sit. It meant a roof over his head, and Stone accepted. The friends, a childless couple, owned a Siamese cat that was not only the apple of their eyes but the whole damn orchard.

Having given exquisitely detailed instructions for the care and feeding of Dingaling — fresh chicken livers, sautéed lightly in equal parts of butter and sherry, two large mushroom caps — and having left behind $35 to purchase the livers from the best butcher, the couple set sail for Le Havre.

Seth went out at once and spent the $35 on cigarettes and beer. Now they were penniless.

During the first week, the cat sulked and refused to eat all but a mouthful or two of the canned sardines and tuna Stone found in the pantry, and scratched earth over the scraps from the refrigerator.

During the second week, the cat changed its tune and ate anything, but there was little of that.

By the third week, they were totally out of food, and the cat, desperate, would have eaten paint off the walls.

Stone was able to cadge an occasional meal for himself from a friend, and there was always the promise of a Salvation Army handout, but the cat was in Hard Luck City. It complained day and night, as only a Siamese can.

On the morning that the owners were to arrive back home, Stone took his first long look at the cat. What a mess! Dull eyes, uncared-for coat, and its ribs sticking out six inches on either side. It looked as though it hadn't had a meal in a week, which it hadn't. It dawned on Stone that he was about to face a firing squad. The minute those people came bursting through the door yelling for kitty, and saw the pathetic broken creature it had become, Stone's life wouldn't be worth a telephone slug. He had to do some fancy dancing, and fast. Racing through the kitchen, he began flinging the cupboard doors open, the cat howling plaintively at his heels. Not one sardine, not even a Ritz cracker. In rising panic, Stone made for the freezer. Empty, except for two packages of frozen green beans. It was time for desperate measures. He ripped open the packages, put the beans up to boil, and poured the cooling mess into the cat's dish. Dingaling fell on the saucer and wolfed down the beans.

As soon as it had eaten, it became a different cat. Its sides filled out; its fur took on a sheen. It was a Siamese again, not a piece of Bowery rubbish.

On cue, the door was flung open and in rushed the couple, calling for their pet, falling on its neck with little whimpers of adoration.

"She looks terrific! Did she give you any trouble?"

"Are you kidding? She and I are the best of friends. Chicken livers every day at ten o'clock, just as you ordered."

That mendacious bastard! If looks could kill, Dingaling would have fried Stone where he stood.

Instead, the cat gave a long shudder, one mighty convulsive heave, and threw up two packages of frozen green beans.

In the not-yet-precise science of predicting earthquakes, cats are proving surprisingly useful. Seismologists have noticed that, about ten days before a quake is due, cats begin to run away from home. Changes in the earth's gravity apparently move the magnetite in their bodies. Before the large Italian earthquake a few years ago, mother cats in the vicinity of the imminent quake began moving their litters to safety. By the time of the quake, there were no cats left. The Chinese are conducting a joint study program with the United States, using animal behavior as one element in quake prediction. Changes in subterranean sounds, water levels, and animal behavior are being minutely recorded. The U.S. Geological Service is operating an Earthquake Watch Hotline, staffed by 1,700 volunteers, along the West Coast. The volunteers chart the behavior of their animals on a daily basis, and call the hot line number to report aberrations that might precede a major earthquake.

"Puss in Boots" is a very old story, older than its first appearance in print, "Le Chat Botté," by Charles Perrault (1697). The tale of an ingenious, clever, and loyal cat who helps his impoverished master to gain a fortune and a royal bride was also told in Italian, where Puss was known as "Constantine's Cat," and in a German play, *Der gestiefelte Kater,* by Ludwig Tieck (1797).

Gustave Doré

Laura Torbet

THE SIAMESE

The Siamese cat was invented by God, who gave it "the grace of the panther, the affection of a love-bird, the beauty of the fawn, the softness of dawn, the swiftness of light." Until 1885, only the royalty of Siam could breed Siamese cats; for two hundred years they could be found only in the Royal City of Bangkok, in the royal court quarters, where they were fed on choice morsels and kept in gold cages before which incense burned. When a member of the royal family died, a live cat was placed in his tomb. A small hole was left in the roof; if the cat wriggled out of the hole, it was believed that the soul of the royal personage had passed into it, and the cat was led into the temple with honors. (As late as 1926, at the coronation of the King of Siam, a white cat was brought into the throne room in procession to symbolize the presence (and possibly the soul) of the departed king.) In 1884, the wife of the British consul general Owen Gould managed to bring a mated pair of Siamese cats home to England, an unprecedented gift from the king. When the breeding cats left the country, the Siamese people wailed in dismay, believing that the cats' departure marked the beginning of the downfall of Siam. At the First National Cat Show in London, at the Crystal Palace in 1871, a contemporary journalist noted that one breed was "an unnatural, nightmare kind of cat" — the Siamese.

How did the Siamese cat come by its crossed eyes? An ancient folk tale tells of a tipsy monk who wandered away from the temple in which was kept enshrined the beautiful golden goblet from which the god Buddha was said to have slaked his thirst. There were two temple cats on duty, and, while one of them went off to find another monk to guard the temple, the second cat remained to keep watch over the precious goblet. She stared at it so long that her eyes crossed. Then, when she was so tired that she fell asleep, she slept with her tail curled tightly around the goblet, so tightly that when she awoke, her tail was permanently kinked. Ever since, Siamese cats wear crossed eyes and kinked tails as a sign of devotion to Buddha.

Here's another explanation of how the kink appeared in the Siamese's tail. A Siamese princess, about to bathe, took off her rings and threaded them onto her cat's tail. But the cat lost the rings. The next time she bathed, the angry princess placed her rings on the tail again, but this time she tied a knot in it, and the tail has been kinked ever since.

Some Siamese cats have two darker markings on either side of their necks. These are called "the temple marks," and show the fingerprints of a god who once picked the cat up by the scruff.

MORE SUPERSTITIONS

The Chinese consider cats to be lucky, because the glow in their eyes can put evil spirits to flight. It's very unlucky to have a cat stolen from a house. Yet, at the same time, there can be ill luck associated with cats. A Chinese author wrote, "the coming of a cat to a household is an omen of approaching poverty. The coming of a strange cat, and its staying in a house, is believed to foreshadow an unfavorable change in the pecuniary condition of the family." The supposition is that the approaching cat can foresee where it will find an abundance of rats and mice, following the downfall of the family fortunes.

 From East Anglia comes the tale of a witch who called up a storm that destroyed the fishing fleet. Now she haunts the fleet in the shape of a cat, which is why, to this day, sailors throw a little part of their catch back into the sea, "for the cat."

 All ship's cats, regardless of sex, are said to be named "Minnie."

During World War II an English officer in Burma painted white cats on army vehicles and kept white cats in the army camp. The Burmese, cat worshippers, believed that the gods were on the British side and supported them against the Japanese.

Just as actors are never supposed to invoke the name *Macbeth* (they refer to it as "The Play"), so sailors believe that one should never say the word "cat," although many are fond of cats and all ships carry them.

An old belief in Brittany is that in the tail of every pure black cat there is one white hair. If you find it, and can pull it out without getting scratched, and can keep it safe, it will bring you good luck.

In Old England, folk belief had it that the cat had the power to cure not only sties, but blindness and other eye diseases. And in Cornwall, the black cat's tail was also effective against skin complaints, particularly warts. Skin disease in the Netherlands, too, was "cured" by applying the skin of a cat to the afflicted places. In Russia, a catskin was placed upon the belly to cure bellyache and cramps.

BORN BLIND

In Scotland, when somebody is talking madness or nonsense, you say "cast the cat over him," meaning that throwing a cat over a madman will restore him to his senses.

Sailors hold an ancient belief that, if a cat is thrown overboard, it presages a shipwreck, nine years of bad luck, and other calamities. There is a sailor's tradition that four things were certain bad luck on an ocean voyage—a black cat on board, a pregnant woman, a clergyman, or sailing on Friday. Howey links this supersitition to an ancient belief in Freya (the Norse goddess of love and fertility for whom Friday was named, and who was always accompanied by two cats) and that her evocation by cats, religious symbols, fertility, or Friday summoned the goddess and left the ship vulnerable to the forces of nature.

There's an old Scots belief that somewhere in the Scottish highlands exist elfin cats as big as dogs. They are black with white chests, and their whiskers are permanently erect. In fact, the European wild cat, bigger than the house cat, is still alive and well in Scotland.

If a cat ate the eyes of a corpse in Scotland it was believed to inflict blindness on the first person it jumped over.

An old peasant belief in many parts of the world: To prevent a cat from running away from home, butter its paws.

Celts believe that cats born in May will bring snakes into the house. In Sussex, England, the May cat superstition is a bit more elaborate. Cats born in May will not catch mice, but bring snakes and glowworms into the house; they are also subject to fits of melancholia.

The Japanese used to believe that the cat had power to cure fits, epilepsy and melancholy. Certainly, a playful and loving cat is the best specific against melancholy ever invented.

In old China, cats were believed to have the power of recalling souls from the dead, of bringing a corpse back to life and turning it into a zombielike creature. Therefore, the Chinese kept their cats away from unburied bodies.

Another superstition connected with death is that if a cat jumps over a coffin that has a body in it, the dead person's soul is in danger unless the cat is killed immediately.

An old Chinese belief: A light-haired cat will bring its owner silver; a dark-haired cat will bring its owner gold.

Gottfried Mind, a Hungarian painter (1768–1814) who lived in Bern, Switzerland, painted cats, bears, and groups of children. He was called "The Raphael of Cats." During an outbreak of rabies in Bern, many cats, including pets, were put to death, and Mind was forced to hide his own pet, Minette. The whole business distressed him so much that he spent the entire following winter sitting by his fireside, carving bears and cats out of chestnuts. The chestnuts became much sought after, but, alas, after twenty years they had all rotted away.

In Christian art, cats have been seen in opposite roles. In Albrecht Dürer's engraving *Adam and Eve,* the cat is depicted honorably, as a symbol of married happiness; there's a cat as part of Barocci's *Holy Family;* Rembrandt also included the cat in his studies of the Holy Family. But in the paintings of Ghirlandaio, Gellini, and Luini that depict The Last Supper, a cat is present at the feet of or by the side of Judas Iscariot, as the living representation of treachery and evil, a foreshadowing of Judas' betrayal of Jesus.

The Meatless Lunch, by Alexandre-François Desportes

So many painters and sculptors have depicted cats that one would need a separate volume just to talk about them all. Steinlen, an Art Nouveau painter, created some of the most famous cats in art with his poster advertisements for milk. Cats have sat for portraits by Leonardo da Vinci, Ingres, Manet, Picasso, Renoir, Hiroshige, Gauguin, Jan Steen, Leonor Fini, Delacroix, Géricault, Hogarth, and many, many others.

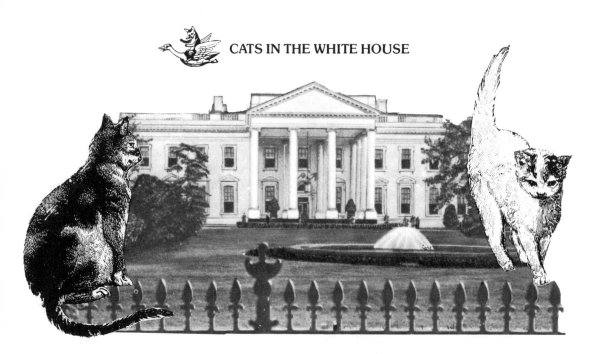

Although "Him" and "Her," President Lyndon Johnson's beagles, made headlines when Johnson demonstrated to the world how he picked them up by the ears, and although Vice-President Nixon's cocker spaniel will live in history, thanks to Nixon's televised "Checkers" speech, dogs are not the only animal inhabitants of the White House. Cats have long been in honored residence there. Even before the White House was built, Martha Washington had a cat door cut into the door of her bedroom at Mount Vernon, so that her cats could enjoy easy ingress and egress.

Presidential daughters seem to prefer cats. Both Susan Ford and Amy Carter owned Siamese cats—Susan's was named Shan, and Amy's rejoiced in the name of Misty Malarky Ying Yang.

Another White House cat was Tom Kitten, Caroline Kennedy's pet. He was named after the famous children's book by Beatrix Potter, who was also the author of *Peter Rabbit*.

Slippers, a cat with extra toes, was one of Theodore Roosevelt's pet cats during his administration as President. The other was Tom Quartz, named for a cat in Mark Twain's *Roughing It.*

The kittens had been housed in General Ulysses S. Grant's tent. On the steamer going back to Washington, President Lincoln decided that the kittens would be inappropriate to the White House, and suggested they be left on the steamer as mousers. But Tad, overhearing sailors grumbling that cats were bad luck, was afraid the kittens would be thrown overboard once the presidential party had disembarked. So Lincoln wrote a presidential order that the three were to be the official mousers of the *River Queen*. Regardless of the President's feelings, Tad *did* keep a cat in the White House. Its name was Tabby.

Abraham Lincoln's son Tad adopted three kittens while touring the battlefields with the President toward the end of the Civil War.

THE CAT IN LEGEND

A touching legend about the origin of the pussywillow tree comes from Poland: A litter of kittens was once thrown into the river to drown. The willows, seeing the cat mother crying on the bank for her kittens, took pity, and dragged their low branches in the water for the kittens to cling to. Since then, the pussywillow trails its branches in the water and every spring puts out little "kittens" of velvet furriness.

There is a farmer's belief in Lorraine, France, that we owe the corn to the cat. It seems that the ear of corn once grew huge, taking up the entire stalk from bottom to top. The farmers used to reserve the top part of the ear, right under the silk, for the cat. God, wishing to punish the evil in man, decreed that the corn plant would henceforth grow only inedible straw. But the angels protested — did God wish to punish the innocent cat along with wicked man? God conceded, and allowed the stalk grow long and the ear short, preserving the cat's portion (which, of course, the cat then lost to man).

There are over three hundred churches on the Greek island of Mykonos, and the smallest of them is barely large enough for one person. It was built by a poor fisherman who, when caught in a storm, prayed to the Virgin, promising Her that if his life was spared he would build a church to Her. After coming safely to shore, he set about building the promised church, although he could afford to build only a tiny one. But when it was finished, the parish priest refused to bless it or to acknowledge it as a place of worship. The fisherman went home and prayed once more to the Virgin. On going back to his little church in the morning, he discovered that a cat had taken up residence there in the night and had given birth to a litter of kittens. The fisherman carried the news to the priest, who accepted it as a sign from the Virgin, and blessed the tiny structure. The church is known even today as "The Virgin of the Cat."

 **SHORT TAKES**

Arthur Rackham

Marine insurance doesn't cover cargo damage by rats, but if the owner of the damaged merchandise can show that the ship set sail without a cat on board, he may be able to recover damages from the shipowner. If a ship is deserted it can be claimed as salvage, but only provided that no living creature is aboard. Many boats have escaped being salvaged because the deserting crew left the ship's cat behind.

The so-called Australian cat wasn't. There are no cats native to Australia, the only continent apart from Antarctica without an indigenous feline population. In the late 1890s, a breed of "Australian cat" was exhibited in the United States, and took many prizes, but the breed resulted from a mutation from a Siamese cat brought there from Great Britain. Unfortunately, the breed was not hardy, and because of its delicacy it soon died out.

The cat is the longest-lived animal of all domesticated species; twenty is not an uncommon age for a cat, and many cats live even twenty-two or twenty-five years. *The Guinness Book of World Records,* 1982 edition, reports that the oldest cat ever recorded was probably "Puss" of Devon, England, who cele-, brated his thirty-sixth birthday on November 28, 1939, and died the next day. "Ma," also of Devon, was put to sleep November 5, 1957, age thirty-four. There must be something in the Devon air, the water, or even the mice, that is salubrious to felines.

The Kit-Cat Club, a famous Whig meeting place in eighteenth-century London whose members included Congreve, Addison and Steele and other literary and political notables, was not named for a cat, but for mutton pies served there. They were called kit-cats possibly in honor of their purveyor, pastry cook Christopher Catt.

Burmese cats originally belonged to the aristocrats and the priests of Burma and could not be sold. Each cat was attended by its own servant.

In 1838, on the evening of the death of Sir Robert Grant, British Governor of Bombay, a cat was seen to leave Government House near Poona, and walk up and down the garden paths, exactly where and how the governor had walked every evening at sunset. The native sentries, beholding this, became instantly convinced that the spirit of Sir Robert had entered into the body of the cat. For twenty-five years after, the sentries would present arms to any cat walking out the front door of Government House.

Tabby markings are genetically dominant over black coats, and short hair is dominant over long. When cats revert to the wild and become feral and breed, they not only breed larger, stronger, and more ferocious kittens, but the fur reverts to tabby, no matter what the color of the antecedents.

The reason a cat's hair stands on end when he confronts an enemy is to make him look larger and more threatening.

Sir Isaac Newton is said to have invented the cat door for the convenience of his pet cats.

In Ancient Egypt they mummified not only cats but also mice, to provide food for the cats in the Afterlife.

There are more wild cats in Scotland today than at any other time within living memory. They are expert fishermen, and live mostly on fish they catch themselves.

A group of cats is a clowder, and a group of kittens is a kendle.

Black-and-white cats are called Magpies by breeders and showers.

Every claw on a cat's paw points in the same direction, which is why a cat can only back down out of a tree, which is in turn why so many of them need the Fire Department to get them down.

 **SHORT TAKES**

Cats are not afraid of water, and they swim perfectly well, in something akin to a dog-paddle, but infinitely more graceful, of course. In fact, a number of South American jungle cats are superb swimmers and have been asked to endorse swimsuits. Turkish cats enjoy water so much that they are known as the "swimming cats."

 Angora cats were probably the first long-haired cats introduced into Europe, brought there by Turkish traders from Ankara, the capital of Turkey, which was then called Angora. Persian cats came, if you can believe it, from Persia, and breeders preferred their round flat faces and cobby bodies to the Angoras, so the latter breed suffered a decline for many years, but is once again on the rise.

When George IV was still Prince of Wales, he was walking down the Strand one early spring morning with a friend when he made a bet with his pal that he would see more cats on the right-hand side of the street than his friend would on the other. The prince won his bet because, wise in the ways of cats, he had chosen to bet on the sunny side of the street.

144

"PLUCKY" LINDBERGH
Ready to "Hop Off".

Contrary to some accounts, Charles Lindbergh did not have a cat with him on his celebrated solo flight across the Atlantic in 1927. For one thing, he eliminated every ounce of unneccessary weight to make the plane as light as possible. Even a passenger weighing only a few pounds was excess baggage. Earlier than the flight, Lucky Lindy was photographed with a tabby kitten in the cockpit of his plane, *Spirit of St. Louis.* The kitten's name was Patsy, and Lindy stated that he didn't take her along with him because it was "too dangerous a journey to risk the cat's life." A one-peseta stamp commemorating the mighty achievement was issued by Spain in 1930. In the upper left hand corner of the stamp was Lindbergh's portrait; the sea ran along the bottom; in the center was the Statue of Liberty, in the upper right, the *Spirit* aloft. And, in the bottom right corner of the stamp sits a cat, watching the plane.

It is not a myth that white-haired, blue-eyed cats are often deaf. Charles Darwin was one of the earliest scientists recording his observation of the phenomenon, which is due to a genetic linkage. Many white cats possess one blue eye and one yellow, nature's way of guarding against deafness. Deaf white parents can transmit deafness to their kittens. As for the hearing of normal cats, it extends beyond human range into higher frequencies, which may explain why cats appear to respond better to women's voices than to men's.

The cat walks or runs by moving first the front and back legs on one side, then those on the other. The only other animals to move in the same way are the camel and the giraffe.

The ears of a cat contain thirty muscles, those of a human, only six. That's why they can rotate their ears, and we can't.

At the disastrous first performance of Rossini's opera, *The Barber of Seville,* a cat walked onstage, turning the boos into laughter and bringing down both the house and the curtain.

A Welsh law, from about the tenth century, says that: "This is a complement of the legal hamlet: nine buildings, one plough, one kiln, one churn, and one cat, one cock, one bull, and one herdsman."

  Catgut for violin strings is actually made from sheepgut. The name "catgut" may have derived from the archaic English word "kit," meaning fiddle. "Kitgut," therefore "catgut." The only instrument actually made with catgut is the Japanese samisen, a stringed instrument traditionally played by geishas. Recently, a group of geishas in Tokyo subscribed for a mass to be said for cats who died in order to furnish them with samisens.

At one time Florence Nightingale owned more than sixty cats! In her later years, she never traveled without one.

The first photographer of cats was Charles Bullard, a New Englander, who began to take their pictures around 1887.

Igor Stravinsky wrote a musical composition, *Berceuses du Chat,* in which the clarinets imitated the voices of cats.

In 1815 in Chester, England, just before the banishment of Napoleon Bonaparte to St. Helena, a practical joker issued a handbill saying that St. Helena was overrun by rats, and that cats would be sent there, to be purchased at sixteen shillings for adult toms, ten shillings for adult tabbies, two shillings and sixpence per kitten that could feed itself. (Napoleon was a notorious ailurophobe; he was so terrified of cats that he sweated mightily in their presence, and one night, shortly after the Battle of Wagram, an aide heard him screaming for help in the middle of the night, and found him lunging with his sword at a tapestry behind which a cat was cowering. He would shudder at the very mention of the word "cat.") On the day appointed for the "sale," Chester was choked with men, women, and children, all carrying cats. A riot ensued, during which the cats escaped, and for weeks the town was overrun by cats, some of whom were killed.

There was a radio program in Great Britain, *Desert Island Discs,* on which celebrities told what they'd take to a desert island if they were cast away. Christopher Milne (the original Christopher Robin of *Winnie the Pooh* fame) declared that he would bring a pregnant cat.

The first pair of Burmese cats in Europe were a gift from temple priests to a British Army major, Russell Gordon, in 1919. Gordon had helped in putting down an uprising in Burma that had threatened the temple, the priests, and the sacred cats.

A male god in the form of a cat, Ai Apaec, was worshiped by the ancient tribe of the Mochicas in Peru.

In Norse mythology the Fenris Wolf, who was fated at birth to destroy the gods, is bound by a silken ribbon made of six impossible things. One of them is the sound of a cat's footfall.

Charles Henry Ross, in his *Book of Cats* (1868) tells the story of a cat who lived in a monastery, where every day he was fed directly after the tolling of the dinner bell. One day, he was accidentally shut into a room when the bell rang, and missed his dinner. After the monks had eaten, they discovered puss and let him out. A minute or so later, they heard the clangor of the bell, went to investigate, and there was the cat, hanging on the rope!

Martial, the first century B.C. Roman epigrammatist, claimed that the first domesticated cats came from Pannonia, which is presently Hungary.

Early Buddhism wasn't overly fond of the cat, as legends show. There is a Chinese legend that the cat is not included among the animals in the Chinese zodiac because she killed a rat at Buddha's funeral, when all animals were supposed to have been at peace. (The cat *is* included in the Vietnamese zodiac; its year corresponds with the Chinese Year of the Rabbit. The last Year of the Cat was 1975; the next will be 1987. People born in the Year of the Cat are "refined, virtuous, lovers of tradition, discreet, clever, altruistic.")

Other legends tell us that the cat was not at Buddha's funeral at all; its presence was forbidden because the cat had failed to weep at Buddha's death, or because it had killed the rat who had been sent to bring the medicine to save Buddha's life. Yet another legend tells us that the cat was the only animal not to escort Buddha to his entrance into Nirvana—it fell asleep halfway there. In any event, the cat was so bum-rapped that Indian Buddhists, preaching love for all creatures, would add, "except the cat."

ALL this trouble might have been avoided by the use of one FIFTEEN CENT BOX of "ROUGH ON RATS." Clears out Rats, Mice, Flies, Bed-Bugs, Ants, Roaches, Mosquitoes, &c.

 **THE WORKING CAT**

A British firm called Shepherd & Sons Ltd. of Burscough, Lancashire, made it into the *Guinness Book of World Records* when it kept a tally of the mice killed by its working cat, a tabby named Mickey. Mickey, who died in 1968, worked for the company twenty-three years, and did away with a recorded number of over 22,000 mice.

No account of working cats can be complete without a salute to Morris, the chubby, cynical marmalade tom who hawks Nine Lives cat food on television. The original Morris, who has passed to his reward, and is now eating lamb chops in Heaven, was snatched from imminent and untimely death when a Chicago shelter was about to have him put down, and went on to fame and fortune as the most finicky animal in creation. Another Morris has, of course, taken his place, spelled now and then by Sylvester, the nasty, lisping, black-and-white animated cartoon cat from Warner Brothers. One wonders whether there are more cats named Morris in America than there are dogs named Snoopy.

The Stafford Hotel in London's Mayfair has become a very popular caravan stop with members of New York's book publishing scene on business in London. Part of the hotel's charm and ambience is the presence of two working cats, Whisky and Soda, who patrol the lobby, looking the guests over. These cats have become almost equal in importance to Hamlet, the famous lobby cat of the Algonquin Hotel in New York.

In 1949 a cat named Ninety worked in the office of the engineers who were building a $6 million bridge across the Connecticut River at Old Lyme. Rats were chewing at the plans and blueprints for the bridge (called Project 90) and it was Ninety who killed the rodents and kept the plans safe. As a reward, when the bridge was opened officially, with great ceremony, it was Ninety who was selected to lead the parade across it.

In 1949, a cat named Solomon worked for Harvey Cunningham, customs inspector at the Texas/Mexico border town of Zapata. Solomon was used to sniff the luggage, the automobiles, and so forth of travelers crossing the border, ferreting out contraband. No, not marijuana, but fresh-killed game.

Charles H. Bennett

 THE CAT IN LITERATURE

One of Aesop's most celebrated fables tells of a rather dim puss who was exploited by a clever monkey; from it we get the expression "cat's paw," meaning one who is made use of to his own disadvantage. In 1857 Charles H. Bennett published in England his own re-telling of Aesop, in witty fables and charming illustrations, and herewith Bennett's version of the fable.

"A cunning old Ape who felt his mouth water at the vicinity of certain tempting fruits which he longed to possess, but which he knew to be guarded in a place too warm for his fingers to venture in, asked a foolish young Cat, whom he saw passing, to come to his assistance.

"'I pray you,' he said, 'lend me your paw to reach those pretty nice things that I require. I am a poor old creature that cannot help himself, and will well reward you for your pains.'

"The silly Cat complied; but in so doing, burnt his claws so terribly that he was unable to catch mice for months to come, while the old Ape got safely off with the plunder.

"MORAL: In the trade of chestnut-stealing, it is the Cat who comes in for the kicks, while the Monkey enjoys the halfpence."

When Mary Hemingway designed a three-storey stone tower at her home, the Finca Vigia in Cuba, in 1947, she intended the structure to fulfill three purposes: to give her husband, novelist Ernest Hemingway, a private place to write, herself a place to sunbathe in the nude, and the Hemingway pet cats—thirty in number—a room of their own that would keep them out of the Finca. Nevertheless, a handful of them retained house privileges and were always underfoot. The rest appeared to like their new quarters, and settled happily into them.

The celebrated choreographer George Balanchine has stated more than once that he prefers cats to people. He taught his cat Mourka to do *jetés* and *tours en l'air,* leaps and turns of classical ballet. His wife, dancer Tanaquil LeClercq, wrote *The Autobiography of a Cat,* the life of the white-and-ginger Mourka. Eyeing his cat with delight and satisfaction, Balanchine declared, "At last! A body worth choreographing for!" In Tchaikovsky's ballet *The Sleeping Beauty* is a *pas de deux* danced by Puss in Boots and the White Cat, while the orchestra imitates cat sounds.

Concert sur les toits, by Coypel

 Edward Lear was passionately devoted to his cat Foss. When a hotel was being built at the bottom of his garden at the Villa Emily in San Remo, Italy, Lear was so offended that he built himself a new home, the Villa Tennyson. The new villa was an exact replica of the Villa Emily, so that Foss would feel at home immediately, and not be made unhappy by the loss of his former home. The pair of them moved in in 1881; when Foss died he was buried in the Villa Tennyson garden. On his grave a tombstone with an inscription in Italian was placed, and Lear himself died soon thereafter.

William Makepeace Thackeray owned a cat named Louisa, whom he fed fish from his own plate.

It was said of Henry James that when he sat down to write, a cat invariably sat on his shoulder. The same is certainly true of Robin Cook, best-selling author of *Coma, Fever,* and other novels. Cook states that his cat sits on his lap or lies on his shoulder every minute he's at the typewriter, contributing its catly consciousness and creativity to the flow of ideas.

Prosper Mérimée, French novelist and man of letters, author of *Carmen,* upon which Bizet based his opera, was a dedicated cat lover, and once wrote, in a letter to a friend, about *un vieux chat noir, parfaitement laid, mais plein d'esprit et de discretion.* There is something most touching about this "old black cat, totally ugly, but filled with spirit and discretion."

Charles Dickens's cat was noted for two widely different reasons. The first was that it would snuff the candle when Dickens was working, jealous of his attention. The second reason was that its name at first was William, but later it had to be re-named Williamina, when "he" presented the famous author with a litter of kittens.

Edgar Allan Poe was cursed by miserable poverty for most of his life. His wife Virginia died of consumption in 1846, as did many of the wretched poor in those days. As she lay dying, the only heat the Poes could afford were his overcoat wrapped around her, Poe holding her hands while her mother clasped her feet to keep them warm, and the large family cat, Catarina, lying on her chest.

THE CAT IN ANCIENT EGYPT

The cat's close identification with the sun in the ancient Egyptian religion is confirmed by the fact that the Egyptian word "mau" means both "cat" and "sun." The sun god, Ra, in the form of a giant cat, fought with the serpent god of darkness, Apep, and killed him.

The Greek historian Herodotus was a fascinated listener to tales of the ancient Egyptians, and much of what we know about Egyptian worship of cats we owe to him. Among the scraps of information he passed along are these: In Egypt it was considered a more heinous crime to kill a cat than to kill a human. Firefighters were obligated, when making fire rescues, to save the household cat or cats first, then the people.

Polyon the Greek philosopher tells us that, when King Cambyses of Persia, son of Cyrus the Great, was besieging the Egyptian garrison at Pelusium in 525 B.C., he resorted to cats to win the city. Knowing the Egyptian reverence for the animal, he had his men scour the surrounding countryside for cats and carry them into the attack in place of shields. The Egyptians threw down their spears, for fear of wounding or killing a cat, and surrendered their city. Much of the same story is told about the siege of Memphis by the Persians a century later—that the Persians used cats in place of stones and catapulted them over the city parapets to the horror of the Egyptian defenders, who surrendered the city lest more cats die.

A CONTEMPORARY CREATION MYTH

Eve and Adam had been living in the Garden of Eden for
about three weeks when Adam asked Jehovah for a pet. "I go
out a lot," he told God, "and I need something to trot along by
my side, fetch sticks, be true blue, and lick my face. Eve isn't
really into any of that."

"Let Me think about it," said God, and went away. When He
came back, He had a dog with Him. "This is Dog," He told
Adam.

The following week, God dropped in on Eve, who was sitting
around scratching aimless circles into the ground with the
pointed end of a stick.

"Oh, I'm all right," she told Jehovah, in answer to His question. "No, no, nothing's the matter. Yes, I love Dog. Dog is very
good for Adam. But if only he . . . oh, nothing."

"No, tell Me," God said, looking concerned.

"Well, Dog is very affectionate. He's a dear, really, but, you
know, he weighs seventy pounds if he weighs an ounce, and
when he climbs up in my lap, it's suffocating. I can't breathe. And
when he licks me with that wet tongue, yeeecccch! And if only he
wasn't so noisy! All day long, bark bark bark, yip yip yelp. Oh, I
don't know. Don't get me wrong, I love Dog, Jehovah, honest!
It's only that sometimes I wish he were smaller, and daintier, and
quieter, and not so damn slobbery!"

"Let Me think about it," said God, and went away. When He came back, He had a cat with Him. "This is Cat," He told Eve.

When Eve saw the pretty little nine-pound animal, she gave a squeal of happiness. "Oh, she's gorgeous! She's exactly what I had in mind. Is she really mine?"

"Really yours," said God.

"Forever and ever?"

"Forever and ever."

And Cat smiled and purred, and wound her dainty body around Eve's legs. And Eve bent and stroked the silky head and gathered Cat up in her arms and cradled her, and they lived happily together forever and ever.

And God saw that it was good, and He was satisfied. Well, almost satisfied. Well, to tell the truth, He was a little unhappy about it all. You see, He had intended to keep Cat for Himself.

A CAT & DOG LIFE.

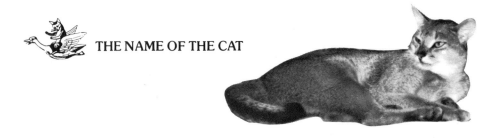

THE NAME OF THE CAT

Writing his natural history in 1607, Edward Topsell had this to say about how the cat got its name:

The Nature and Etymology of a Cat

A Cat is a familiar and well known beast, called of the Hebrews *Cattus*, and *Schanar*, and *Schundra*; of the Grecians, *Aeluros*, and *Kattes*, and *Katis*; of the Saracens, *Katt*; the Italians, *Gatta*, and *Gatto*; the Spaniards, *Gata* and *Gato*; the French, *Chat*; the Germans *Katz*; the Illyrians, *Kozka* and *Furioz* (which is used for a cat by Albertus Magnus) and I conjecture, to be either the Persian or the Arabian word. The Latins call it *Feles*, and sometimes *Murilegus*, and *Musto*, because it catcheth Mice, but most commonly *Catus*, which is derived of *Cautus*, signifying wary. Ovid saith, that when the Giants warred with the Gods, the Gods put upon them the shapes of Beasts, and the sister of Apollo lay for a spy in the likeness of a Cat, for a Cat is a watchful and wary beast seldom overtaken, and most attendant to her sport and prey.

In Arabic, the word for cat is *kittah; Webster's Third New International Dictionary* gives the origin of the word "cat" thus: from "Middle English *cat, catte,* from Old English *catt, catte;* akin to Old Frisian *kate;* Old High German *kazza,* Old Norse köttr; all from a prehistoric North Germanic–West Germanic word, probably borrowed from Late Latin *cattus, catta,* perhaps of Hamitic origin; akin to Berber *kaddiska,* cat, Nubian *kadis.*" What a lesson in the history of cats is there! From North Africa, the name spread to the Roman Empire, from the Romans to the Gauls and the Germans, from there to the Scandinavian countries, thence to England.

Although its incredible speed makes it a formidable hunter, the cheetah is, when not hungry, quite an amiable animal and makes a pretty good pet. Not in a one-bedroom apartment, of course. The cheetah was, in fact, domesticated by the ancient Egyptians, and wall paintings dating back to 1500 B.C. show it being led on a leash and used in the hunt. In the middle ages, they were kept for hunting by Mongol princes, and they are still being imported from Africa for use by the East Indian nobility in the hunt. In the *Iliad,* Homer's warriors rode to the battle in their chariots, then dismounted and fought on foot. So it is with the cheetah, which, blindfolded, is brought to the chase by vehicle, usually a jeep; the blindfold is removed when the quarry is sighted and the cheetah is let loose.

 **CATS IN THE NEWS**

In June of 1949, the Illinois State Legislature passed the "Marauding Cat Bill," which called for cat owners to be fined for letting their cats run free, and which permitted the capture of cats by police and other citizens and allowed the use of traps. The wording of the bill accused cats of being public nuisances that destroy songbirds. Bascom Timmons, the Washington newsman and former honorary president of National Cat Week, who owned the cat that had the crush on Calvin Coolidge's canary, headed the drive for a veto. The governor of Illinois then was Adlai Stevenson, owner of Muffy, a cat. Stevenson vetoed the bill, with the words, "It is in the nature of cats to do a certain amount of unescorted roaming . . . The problem of cat versus bird is as old as time. If we attempt to resolve it by legislation, who knows but what we may be called upon to take sides as well in the age-old problems of dog versus cat, bird versus bird, even bird versus worm. In my opinion, the State of Illinois and its local governing bodies already have enough to do without trying to control feline delinquency." Within the year, Adlai Stevenson had won the annual *Cat Magazine* award for "the Great Veto" of the Marauding Cat Bill. In its editorial, *Cat* averred that the bill "had its inception as a result of a well organized group of cat haters with financial backing from *every* section of the United States." Stevenson went on to twice win the Democratic Party nomination for presidential candidate, and twice go down to defeat at the hands of Dwight D. Eisenhower.

There's a military graveyard for pets in Fort Monroe, Virginia, in which are buried hundreds of cats, dogs, canaries, hamsters, rabbits, and other animals. The bereaved are military personnel of the U.S. services, both active-duty and retired, many of whom have traveled hundreds, even thousands of miles to give Fluff or Bowser a patriotic resting place. Grave markers range from simple wooden crosses to rather elaborate marble mausoleums. (In the case of a pet rodent, would that be *mouseoleum*?)

In November of 1964, the Dutch Embassy in Moscow discovered that they were being bugged by the Russians. Microphones had been buried in the walls, and when activated their very slight sound was inaudible to humans. The embassy's two Siamese cats, however, with their super-sensitive ears, detected the sounds, and kept meowing and clawing at the walls until their owners had them excavated, expecting mice, but finding mikes. The Dutch, a calm and phlegmatic people, made no undue fuss about the microphones, but did use them to register their complaints about the embassy building to their landlords, the Russians.

 **A LOVELY LEGEND**

Why does Japanese art so frequently depict the good-luck cat with its right front paw raised up to the level of its ear? This cat, Maneki-Neko, sits in the window of almost every Japanese restaurant in the world and on the doorstep of houses, inns, bathhouses, and other places that welcome the traveler. Her image is painted all over the facade of the temple of Go-To-Ku-Ji in Tokyo, and effigies of the same seated cat figure, paw raised, are everywhere around the temple.

The answer is this lovely legend. The temple of Go-To-Ku-Ji was once very poor, not rich as it is today. But it did have a temple cat. One day, as the cat was washing her face, a band of samurai was riding by. They saw the little cat with her paw raised to her ear; interpreting this as a beckoning welcoming gesture, they rode into the temple courtyard. There they were greeted warmly, and pressed to stay for tea. The samurai remained to speak of Buddhism with the priest and one of them, a wealthy and powerful man, returned for religious instruction. When he died, he left the temple a huge endowment.

And all because a cat was washing her face! No wonder Maneki-Neko is considered lucky!

Have you ever wondered why dogs can be so different from breed to breed, while all cats are siblings under the skin? If you were a little green Martian and were faced with a St. Bernard and a Mexican hairless, how could you tell they were the same species? On the other hand, if you saw a Siamese and a Persian together, you'd have to be a pretty dim little green Martian not to recognize them both as cats. The main reason is that dogs have been bred for thousands of years, and most of the variations between breeds derive from the unnatural selection of the human race. But, too, cats are not as genetically variable as dogs. You might change a leopard's spots, but not his shape. Except for eye and fur color and length, all cats are basically the same. Orientals are bred for leanness of body, some longhairs for cobbiness, but a cat for all that is a cat. Not only that, but, regardless of the number of breeds and exotic nomenclature, there are only three breeds of cat; in purebred, these are longhair and shorthair. In non-purebred cats, "alley cat" will do, although domestic shorthair is the name we alley-cat owners prefer.

In his seminal work of science *On the Origin of Species* naturalist Charles Darwin wrote of "the balance of nature," pointing out that (a) the visits of bumblebees are necessary for the fertilization of red clover (the bumblebee, by virtue of its size, is the only bee suitable for red clover); (b) the number of bumblebees depends on the number of mice in any given area, since mice destroy honeycombs and hives; (c) the number of mice depends on the number of cats; and (d) it is generally known that bee nests are commonly found in greater numbers near villages and small towns than in open country. Darwin's hypothesis: that (d) is attributable to the people in the towns who keep the cats who keep down the mice, thus allowing the bees to fertilize red clover. Therefore, such a statistic as the size of the cat population feasibly affects the prevalence of flower occurrence in a given area.

How can you tell a baby boy kitten from a baby girl kitten? Admittedly, it's difficult when they are very young. Charles Dickens' William was later rechristened Williamina; many a Sam has had to be called Samantha when the kittens arrived. (Why, the very editor of this book changed his Abyssinian kitten's name from Precious Gold to Hudson when "she" turned out to be "he.") But here's one way to judge gender, although it's not guaranteed foolproof.

Think of punctuation marks. If, when you lift the little tail, you see a wide-apart colon, it's a male. If you see an upside-down exclamation point, you've got a female.

BOY :

GIRL ¡

The earliest book about cats is a collection of poetry from Siam, *The Cat-Book Poems,* which was written between the years 1350–1750. The earliest cat book in prose was *A History of Cats*, published in Paris in 1727 and written by François-Augustin Paradis de Moncrif, who was unmercifully ribbed for the rest of his life for writing a book on such a trivial subject. Wherever he went, he was greeted by meows and kissing calls of "Puss, puss," and he was categorized as *"l'historio griffe,"* or "one who writes the history of the claw." When he was elected at last to the Académie Française, cats were let loose during his inaugural address.

When the writer Petrarch died in 1370, his son-in-law Francesco de Brossano had his pet cat put to death and mummified. It can be seen today in a glass case in a niche in Petrarch's study in the Vaucluse valley in southern France. The niche is decorated with the marble effigy of a cat and an inscription in Latin that says, "Second only to Laura."

The late Dr. Louis J. Camuti was a man in ten million. He was not only a cat doctor exclusively (and author of *All My Patients Are Under the Bed*) but he made house calls! "You can't spell 'Camuti' without a C-A-T," he used to say. For twenty years, Dr. Camuti had one unfulfilled desire — to own a license plate that read "CAT." In the days before vanity plates were allowed in New York and New Jersey, this was an impossible dream — no letters, only numbers were allowed — until Dr. Camuti met up with Phyllis Levy, fiction and fiction books editor of the *Ladies Home Journal*. Dr. Camuti made a house call to Ms. Levy's beloved pet cat, and a friendship ripened between them; at the end of his rounds on Monday, Wednesday, and Friday night, the doctor would take tea with the editor. When Phyllis learned of the doctor's hopeless wish, the license plate, she made up her mind he'd have it if she had to move heaven and earth to get it. Which she did. Having once run a piece of John V. Lindsay's novel in the magazine, she was emboldened to approach the former mayor of New York City. Lindsay agreed to speak to the Commissioner of Motor Vehicles in Dr. Camuti's behalf. On the night that the precious license plate was presented to the doctor, Levy threw a huge party, with cat-lovers and Camuti-lovers of every stripe present and beaming. A portrait of Dr. Camuti and his car, the license plate prominent and cats everywhere, was painted by Mimi Vang Olsen and hangs in Phyllis Levy's apartment, a treasured memento of a job well done, a wonderful friendship, and a valuable man.

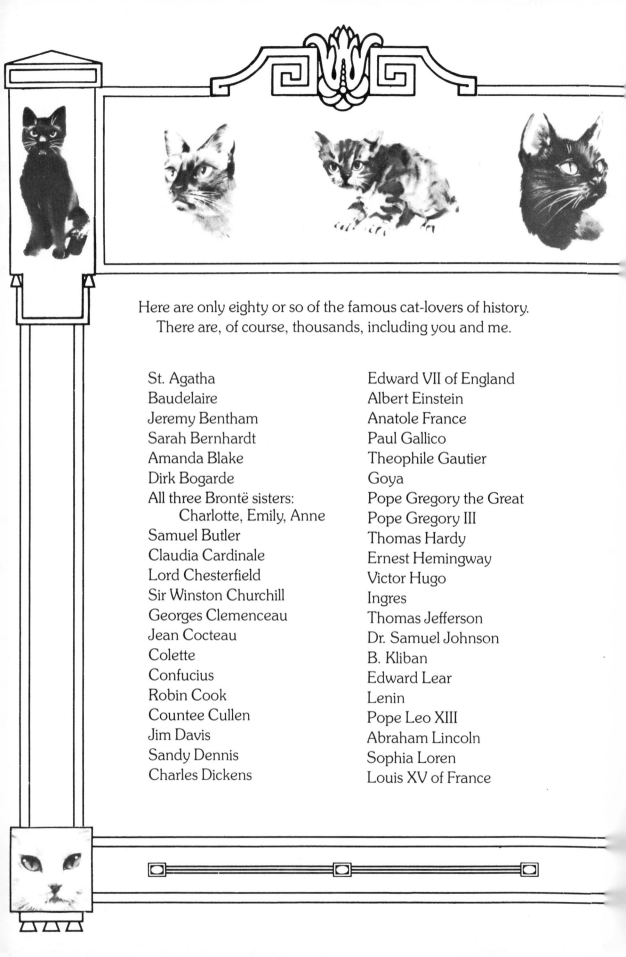

Here are only eighty or so of the famous cat-lovers of history.
There are, of course, thousands, including you and me.

St. Agatha
Baudelaire
Jeremy Bentham
Sarah Bernhardt
Amanda Blake
Dirk Bogarde
All three Brontë sisters:
    Charlotte, Emily, Anne
Samuel Butler
Claudia Cardinale
Lord Chesterfield
Sir Winston Churchill
Georges Clemenceau
Jean Cocteau
Colette
Confucius
Robin Cook
Countee Cullen
Jim Davis
Sandy Dennis
Charles Dickens

Edward VII of England
Albert Einstein
Anatole France
Paul Gallico
Theophile Gautier
Goya
Pope Gregory the Great
Pope Gregory III
Thomas Hardy
Ernest Hemingway
Victor Hugo
Ingres
Thomas Jefferson
Dr. Samuel Johnson
B. Kliban
Edward Lear
Lenin
Pope Leo XIII
Abraham Lincoln
Sophia Loren
Louis XV of France

Anna Magnani
Stephane Mallarmé
Marie Antoinette
Manet
Guy de Maupassant
Montaigne
Muhammed
Sir Philip Neri
Sir Isaac Newton
Florence Nightingale
Peter O'Toole
Louis Pasteur
General George S. Patton
St. Patrick
Jane Pauley
Petrarch
Pablo Picasso
Pope Pius VII
Edgar Allan Poe
Mme. Récamier
Rembrandt

Cardinal Richelieu
Franklin D. Roosevelt
Theodore Roosevelt
Jean-Jacques Rousseau
May Sarton
Albert Schweitzer
George Bernard Shaw
Liz Smith
Mme. de Staël
Steinlen
Elizabeth Taylor
Ellen Terry
Garry Trudeau
Mark Twain
Queen Victoria
Horace Walpole
George Washington
H. G. Wells
Jessamyn West
Cardinal Wolsey
Emile Zola

 ## A FOND FAREWELL

The death of a beloved pet cat is disturbing indeed, but poets feed on the emotions, digesting sorrow and joy with equal pleasure. Many a celebrated poet has been touched by the Muse when a cat dies; here are but a few of the elegies and eulogies resultant.

Pet was never mourned as you,
Purrer of the spotless hue,
Plumy tail, and wistful gaze
While you humored our queer ways,
Or outshrilled your morning call
Up the stairs and through the hall—
Foot suspended in its fall—
While, expectant, you would stand
Arched, to meet the stroking hand;
Till your way you chose to wend
Yonder, to your tragic end . . .
. . . Strange it is this speechless thing
Subject to our mastering,
Subject for his life and food
To our gift, and time, and mood;
Timid pensioner of us Powers,
His existence ruled by ours,
Should—by crossing at a breath
Into safe and shielded death,
By the merely taking hence
Of his insignificance—
Loom as largened to the sense . . .

—Thomas Hardy, *Last Words to a Dumb Friend*

"DOSSIE"

The most famous poetic epitaph was written by the poet Thomas Gray, author of "Elegy in a Country Churchyard." When his close friend, Horace Walpole, wrote Gray that his pet cat, the beloved Selima, had died, Gray penned an ode to the cat, "On the Death of a Favourite Cat Drowned in a Tub of Gold Fishes" which praised Selima's "fair round face, the snowy beard, the velvet of her paws . . . her ears of jet, the emerald eyes" and included the immortal lines, "What female heart can gold despise?/What cat's averse to fish?" The poem began with the lines, " 'Twas on a lofty vase's side/Where China's gayest art had dyed/The azure flowers, that blow; . . ."

Walpole was so enchanted with Gray's poem that he had the actual vase in the first line engraved with the first six lines of the ode, only changing the words "a lofty vase" to "this lofty vase." He kept the vase on a pedestal thereafter.

John Greenleaf Whittier once wrote the following epitaph
for a cat:

Bathsheba: whom none has ever said scat
No worthier cat
Ever sat on a mat
Or caught a rat
Requies-cat.

Which we find a dreadful pun, both in Latin and out of it.

Mike, the working cat of the main gatehouse of the British Museum, was the only creature allowed into the library of the museum without a ticket. His tenure lasted from 1909 to 1921, and when he died, he was the subject of an obituary in the London *Times* written by the eminent Egyptologist Sir Ernest Wallis Budge, and of two memorial poems, one written by F. C. W. Hiley, the assistant keeper of printed books, and one by Dr. Arundell Esdale, the secretary of the museum.

GREAT CAT QUOTATIONS

Life will go on forever
With all that a cat can wish
Warmth, and the glad procession
Of fish and milk and fish.

— Alexander Gray, "On a Cat Aging."